937

Dear Aggie,

I wrote you six letters already. I did not forget you. You forgot me.

I still ... I only picked that b... of the bo... He lives o... in the riv... rd of. Aft... nd you st... nt Roosev... .

P.S. This is letter number seven. I'm keeping track.

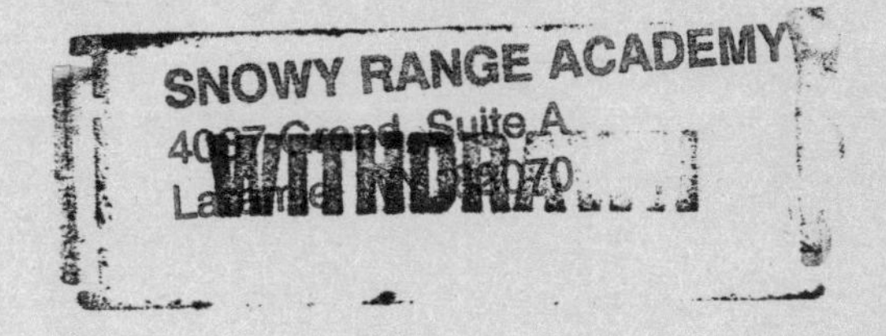

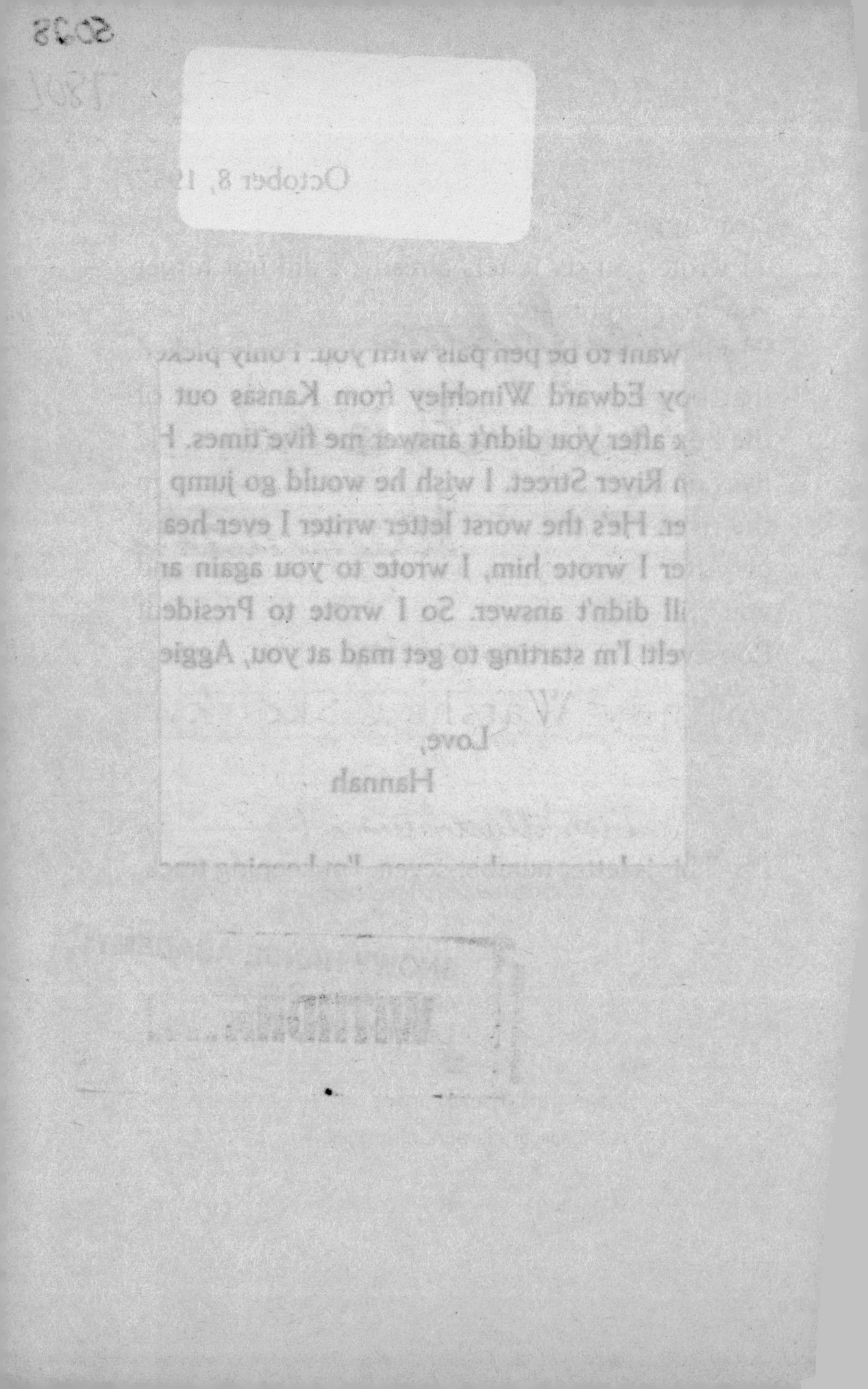

Love from Your Friend, Hannah

a novel by

Mindy Warshaw Skolsky

With illustrations by

Hannah herself

HarperTrophy®
A Division of HarperCollins*Publishers*

Published by arrangement with DK Publishing, Inc.,
an imprint of DK Publishing, Inc., New York

Harper Trophy® is a registered trademark of HarperCollins Publishers Inc.

Love from Your Friend, Hannah
 Printed in the United States of America. For information address HarperCollins Children's Books, a division of HarperCollins Publishers, 10 East 53rd Street, New York, NY 10022.

Library of Congress Cataloging-in-Publication Data
Skolsky, Mindy Warshaw.
Love from your friend, Hannah / a novel by Mindy Warshaw Skolsky ; with illustrations by Hannah herself.
p. cm.
Summary: From her home in back of The Grand View Restaurant in rural New York, Hannah writes letters to her best friend, a pen pal, and even to President and Mrs. Roosevelt.
ISBN 0-06-440746-2
[1. Letters—Fiction. 2. Pen pals—Fiction.] I. Title.
[PZ7.S62836Lo 1999] 99-27015
[Fic]—dc21 CIP

Typography by Jennifer Browne

This work was originally published in 1998 by DK Publishing, Inc.
First Harper Trophy edition, 1999
Visit us on the World Wide Web! http://www.harperchildrens.com

To Bernie,
just because I love you

Love from Your Friend,
Hannah

Hannah Diamond
Route 9W
Grand View, New York

Edward Winchley
37 River Road
Wichita, Kansas

September 27, 1937

Dear Edward,

I got your name and address from a piece of paper I picked out of a box that says PEN PALS on a corner of my teacher's desk. I've never done this before and I don't know exactly what to say. So I'll just pretend I'm talking.

My name is Hannah Diamond, and I live on Route 9W in Grand View, New York. Route 9W is between a mountain and a river. Sometimes I play up on the mountain and other times down by the river. I guess you have a river too, but do you have a mountain?

We have the Grand View Restaurant, with five tables and a counter. Outside is a garage with two gas pumps. Sometimes I help wait on tables, and sometimes I help pump gas.

We live in back of the restaurant. Behind us is a railroad

track, and when the train goes by, everything jiggles. In my room I have the biggest rolltop desk you ever saw. It was here when we bought the restaurant. I like to sit here and write letters and stories and draw pictures. That's my hobby.

I write letters to my grandma and grandpa at their candy store in the Bronx, New York, and I write letters to my best friend, Aggie, who moved the first week of school but so far she doesn't answer, even though I wrote five letters already! That's why I'm looking for a pen pal.

My father makes inventions. He sawed a big hole in the wall and put a giant fish tank into it, with goldfish and snails. You can see it from both sides. The customers see it from the restaurant and we see it from the living room.

Making inventions is my father's hobby.

He invented a hamburger maker that makes twelve hamburgers at a time and a trapdoor in the bathroom that leads to the cellar stairs. He also made the stairs because when we moved in there weren't any. You had to go outside to get to the cellar.

I have a dog, Skippy, who hates to get a bath and always jumps up out of the bucket and runs away covered with soapsuds and gets leaves and pine needles all stuck to him. When he comes home he looks like a porcupine and smells like a skunk.

My mother's hobby is flowerpots.

Grand View doesn't have a school so I go to the Liberty Street School in Nyack. I have to take the school bus, which I hate because the boys on the bus behave like wild animals.

When I picked that piece of paper out of the pen pal

box on my teacher's desk, I really wanted a girl, but my teacher, Miss Hopkins, says you have to take what you get. I got you. I would like a pen pal from Kansas, even though you're a boy, because in my second favorite book, *The Wizard of Oz,* Dorothy lives in Kansas. My first favorite book is *Heidi.*

What are your favorite books?

Your friend,
Hannah Diamond

October 3, 1937

Dear Hannah,
I haven't got a mountain.
I have a cow.

Edward Winchley

P.S. I don't like to read books. I don't like to write letters either. My teacher made me put my name on that piece of paper.

October 6, 1937

Dear Aggie,

On account of you not answering my five letters, listen to what happened to me. I picked a *boy* out of the pen pal box. Miss Hopkins saw me so I couldn't throw him back in. She said if I didn't write to him, I wouldn't be a good sport. So I wrote him a long letter. He wrote me such a dopey letter back, I'm not even going to answer it. Now I could get in trouble with Miss Hopkins if she finds out. She might call me a poor sport in front of the whole class.

Love,
Hannah

P.S. This is my sixth letter, Aggie.

Hannah Diamond
Route 9W
Grand View, New York

President Franklin Delano Roosevelt
The White House
1600 Pennsylvania Avenue
Washington, D.C.

October 7, 1937

Dear President Roosevelt,

I have a problem.

My best friend, Aggie Branagan, moved away. Her father is a wallpaper hanger and he didn't make enough money to pay the rent. He said it was because of hard times.

My mother said it was because he leaves lumps of paste under the paper.

Anyhow, they moved. Mr. Branagan, Aggie's father, drove her up in his wallpaper truck just before they left so she could say good-bye. She cried so hard I felt terrible. I tried to cheer her up. I got an idea: I promised to be her pen pal. She said, "You won't, Hannah—you'll forget about me." I told her, "I'll never forget you, Aggie—you're my best friend." But she still kept crying. So I said, "You know we both always wanted a pen pal, Aggie. Look—I'm running straight to my room to write to you this minute so you'll get my letter right away." And I did.

I wrote a big long letter. The next day I wrote another one. And the day after that. Then I waited and waited, but guess what? She didn't answer! So I still kept writing more letters but she didn't answer those either. Altogether I wrote six letters so far—my mother says I'm using up all the three-cent stamps—but I still haven't got one answer. Not even a penny postcard! And *she* was the one that cried. I was trying to cheer her up. Now I can't even cheer myself up.

In school the teacher has a box on her desk with pieces of paper inside with names of children in other schools. It says PEN PALS on the box. You reach in and pick out a name. I never did it before because you have to take the first name you pick and it might be a boy. Aggie picked one just before she moved and she got a boy. She put it back in the box when the teacher wasn't looking. Also, if you get an answer, you have to read it to the class standing up and I don't like to. I like to read sitting down. But when Aggie didn't answer me five times, I took a chance on the box. Who did I get? Edward Winchley from Wichita, Kansas.

I tried to be nice. I wrote and told him all about my mother, my father, my dog, and the Grand View Restaurant we live in back of, my hobbies—everything I could think of. *Everything!*

I wrote three whole pages.

And do you know what he wrote back? Two measly lines and an unfriendly P.S.

I didn't show it to the teacher. I didn't read it to the class. I was so insulted, I threw it in the garbage.

President Roosevelt, I know you are very busy being our president and trying to fix the hard times, but my father says the reason he voted for you is that you understand the people's problems, and my problem is I haven't got a best friend anymore and I haven't got a pen pal either.

So could you help me find a pen pal?

Love,
Hannah Diamond

October 8, 1937

Dear Aggie,

I wrote you six letters already. I did not forget you. You forgot me.

I still want to be pen pals with you. I only picked that boy Edward Winchley from Kansas out of the box after you didn't answer me five times. He lives on River Street. I wish he would go jump in the river.

He's the worst letter writer I ever heard of.

After I wrote to him, I wrote to you again and you still didn't answer.

So I wrote to President Roosevelt!

I'm starting to get mad at you, Aggie.

Love,
Hannah

P.S. This is letter number seven. I'm keeping track.

October 8, 1937

Dear Grandma,

Remember when I was in the second grade and you and Grandpa moved out here for a year and we played school every day when I came home and I was the teacher? And remember one day I gave you a spelling test with ten words and you said the first nine words were too easy so then I gave you the tenth word, *comb,* and you spelled it *c-o-m.* And we had sort of a little argument because you said *c-o-m-b* was "combuh." Well, I'm sorry I did that, Grandma. My mother said it wasn't fair because you didn't go to school in this country. It was mean.

And remember that same night we went to the carnival in the park down by the river and met my friend Aggie and her father, Mr. Branagan? He wanted to buy me a hot dog and buy you a glass of beer but you said no even though I wanted the hot dog, so we had another little disagreement but then we made up? Well, I'm sorry about that too because I promised not to pester you at the carnival and I did.

But what I really wanted to tell you, Grandma, is Aggie moved! She said she would be my pen pal, but I wrote her seven letters already and she didn't answer one.

I wish you and Grandpa never moved back to the Bronx, New York, but I know it was hard work for Grandpa to take the bus to the city and work in the store all day and then come back here at night.

I miss you a lot though. I miss playing school. I wish you could be the pupil and I could be the teacher again.

I would never give you another hard spelling word like *comb*.

Love,
Hannah

P.S. You'll never guess who I wrote a letter to besides Aggie (not counting a dumb boy from Wichita, Kansas). I wrote to President Roosevelt! I might even write to him again if Aggie doesn't answer soon.

October 10, 1937

Dear President Roosevelt,

Do you like hamburgers?

The Grand View Restaurant has the best hamburgers in the world. My father says so.

With his invention that makes twelve hamburgers at one time, he rolls out the chopmeat with a rolling pin, like cookie dough. Then he takes his invention—like a big tic-tac-toe with twelve squares—and holds it over the rolled-out chopmeat. He brings it down—*bang!*—and when he picks it up, there are twelve hamburgers. He puts them in a pile with waxed paper in between each one. Then he puts them in the refrigerator.

The rolls are round but the hamburgers are square so four corners stick out. My father says customers get four extra bites.

Besides making inventions, my father's other hobby is making signs. He makes every letter out of wood at his worktable in the cellar and I get to help paint them. One sign says A CLEAN LIFE IS A LONG LIFE. KEEP THIS PLACE CLEAN AND LIVE LONGER. I painted both periods. On the roof is the biggest sign. It says GRAND VIEW HAMBURGERS HAVE FOUR EXTRA BITES. THE SQUARE DEAL. I painted the eight E's.

All the customers say our hamburgers are delicious. On the front counter and on the five tables inside we have ketchup, mustard, and pickle relish, so you can put one, two, or three things on top. Also you can have onions and French-fried potatoes and lettuce and tomatoes.

I know Washington, D.C., is far from Grand View, New York, but I wish you could come for a hamburger—

if you like hamburgers, President Roosevelt. I never met anybody who didn't like hamburgers, did you?

But if you don't like hamburgers, we also have hot dogs.

I would wait on you. For a tip, I usually get a nickel or a dime, but you wouldn't have to leave me a tip because you're the president of the United States.

My father says if you came here, he wouldn't charge you anything at all because you made the New Deal to help people who have no work and are poor. He says because of you, my friend Aggie Branagan's father might get more work.

My mother says he better smooth out his lumps though.

Aggie still didn't answer me so I still need a pen pal.

Love,
Hannah

P.S. Do you have a hobby?

October 11, 1937

Dear Hannah,

Grandpa and I were happy you wrote a letter to the president of the United States. We think President Roosevelt is wonderful. We also think you are wonderful.

So come see us.

We'll go to the movies. I'll make you an egg cream. Grandpa will buy you a charlotte russe.

We'll play school again. We'll talk.

You'll feel much better.

Love from your old pupil
who will never forget
how to spell *comb,*
Grandma

October 13, 1937

Dear President Roosevelt,

My teacher says I should tell you something. But first I have to *ask* you something:

Do you know anybody who stands up in bed when they hear "The Star Spangled Banner"?

Last night I got in trouble over it. Not because I stood up for "The Star Spangled Banner" but because I was supposed to be asleep. Also my bed fell apart.

Every Sunday night we listen to Eddie Cantor on the radio. He always makes me laugh and so do the other people on his show. My favorite is Mr. Parkyakarkas. I also like Edgar Bergen and Charlie McCarthy. I know Charlie McCarthy is a dummy but he sounds like a real boy to me. Better than that smart aleck Edward Winchley from Wichita, Kansas. I laugh through the whole show but then at the end when Eddie Cantor sings, "I love to spend each Sunday with you," I start to feel sad. Because then he sings, "As friend to friend, I'm sorry it's through," and then *I'm* sorry it's through too.

It's sad when your friend has to leave. That's how I felt when Aggie Branagan moved away. And I still do because she doesn't answer my letters and be my pen pal. I'm glad *you* are my friend, President Roosevelt. I listened to you on the radio last night with my mother and father. It was a fireside chat but we haven't got a fireplace. We have our great big fish tank though and every night when my father turns on the lights that he put on both sides of it, we watch the goldfish swim around. We have mostly orange, but also black and white. They have pop-eyes and wavy fins. The orange ones are my favorites because underneath the orange is gold. At the bottom of the tank there are colored pebbles and tall grass and a castle that the fish can swim in and out of. And little snails.

My mother doesn't like it because when my father cleans it out he puts all the fish in the bathtub. But my father and I love it.

He says he'd like to have a fireplace to stare into and watch the fire but we don't so the next best thing is to stare into the fish tank and watch the fish. Our radio is next to the fish tank so when you said it was a fireside chat my father said in our house it's a fish-tank chat.

Then you started to talk and you said, "My *friends* . . ." and I got goose bumps! I don't know if it was because your voice is so nice or because you called me your friend. Every time you talk on the radio, I hold my breath until you say "my friends" because I like it so much.

When Eddie Cantor sings, "I love to spend each Sunday with you," I feel like he's my friend too. It's nice to have friends. I love the Grand View Restaurant but it's on a highway and there's nobody around to play with except Skippy, my dog.

Although when I go up on the mountain or down by the river I don't mind being alone. I like it. I have a secret place at the top of the mountain that nobody knows about but me. I think it's the most beautiful place in the world.

Love from your friend,
Hannah

P.S. I forgot to tell you the main thing!

After Eddie Cantor I have to go to bed. I'm supposed to go to sleep. But I only pretend I'm sleeping. I love to listen to the radio. So I listen to whatever my parents are listening to till they turn the radio off.

After the last program, the station always plays "The Star Spangled Banner" and I stand up like you're supposed to when you hear "The Star Spangled Banner." My teacher says so. But late Sunday night I'm too tired to get out of bed and stand on the floor so I stand up in bed. I do it very quietly so my parents won't know I'm still awake. But last night I think I started to fall asleep and when I woke up it was already "By the dawn's early light" so I jumped up very fast—and the slats fell out of my bed. *Klunk!* The whole bed fell down with me in the middle and I got in trouble. My mother said a person should *not* stand up in bed but I told her my teacher said you should always stand for "The Star Spangled Banner." My mother said, "I'm sure your teacher will excuse you if you're already in bed—just ask her." Then my father put the bed back together and when I asked my teacher this morning she said I'm probably the most patriotic person in the whole United States and that's what she said I should tell you.

Love from your patriotic friend,
Hannah

October 15, 1937

Dear Grandma,

Did you and Grandpa listen to President Roosevelt's fireside chat? A funny thing happened to me after it was over. I'll tell you about it when I see you.

I wish I could come see you right now! But if I come now, it can only be for a weekend and that's never long enough. So I was thinking: Christmas vacation is long. If I came then, we could go to the movies two or three times! I don't like to go to the movies alone which is what I've been doing since Aggie Branagan moved away.

When I used to tell Aggie about visiting you, she always said I was lucky I had a grandma and grandpa who owned a candy store. And you know what? She was right. I always wished someday Aggie could come along with me. Now she's ten miles up the river in Haverstraw and I can't even get her to answer a letter.

I'm glad *you* answer letters, Grandma.

I'm also glad I'm still your favorite teacher.

So I'll see you in December but please write me some more letters before then because this is only October.

When I ran up to the top of the mountain today, the trees were all different colors. In my special place I made a great big pile of all the leaves that had fallen on the ground and jumped in them.

Love,
Hannah

P.S. We could still play school in a letter! I could give you Miss Hopkins's new word of the week and you could write it five times and then use it in a sentence the way we do. Our word for this week was: *automobile*.

October 20, 1937

Dear Teacher Hannah,

1. automobile
2. automobile
3. automobile
4. automobile
5. automobile

Sentence: An *automobile* is something I haven't got. First, I can't afford it and second, who needs it? I can take the subway, the bus, or the trolley for a nickel.

Love,
Grandma, your favorite pupil

October 24, 1937

Dear Grandma,

Well, okay for *automobile.* But you wrote three sentences. You only need one. The teacher just wants to make sure we know what the word means.

The word for this week is: *spaghetti.*

Love,
Hannah

October 28, 1937

Dear Hannah,

1. spaghetti
2. spaghetti
3. spaghetti
4. spaghetti
5. spaghetti

Sentence: *Spaghetti* is my granddaughter-teacher's favorite food. Does she like to eat her grandmother's gefilte fish? No. Does she like to eat her grandmother's light and fluffy matzo balls? No. What is the only thing she likes to eat when she comes to see us in the Bronx, New York? *Spaghetti!* With tomato sauce and stinky cheese.

Love,
Grandma

P.S. I didn't forget about just one sentence. But a lot of sentences is more fun. School should be fun.

November 5, 1937

Dear Grandma,

Well, okay about the sentences. I still remember the time I gave you *comb* and you got mad because you said school was no fun and you walked out. So okay if you want school to be fun. You can write all the sentences you want.

The word for this week is: *maraschino cherries*. Miss Hopkins didn't give us that word. I made it up just for you. I'm the teacher again!

Love,
Hannah

P.S. Don't feel bad that I don't like your fluffy matzo balls—I just like hard crunchy ones. But our neighbor, Mrs. Warner, the one who invites me over to listen to the radio with her, *loves* your matzo balls—ever since you gave her a taste last time you were here.

November 10, 1937

Dear Aggie,

Remember in the third grade when the principal was Miss Valentine and we had that special assembly? She made us all sit still and be quiet and listen to a radio speech over the loudspeaker. She said, "Boys and girls, you are going to listen to history!"

And the history was the king of England saying he didn't want to be the king of England. He just wanted to marry "the woman I love." That's what he called her—only he pronounced "love" like this: "lahv." You and I looked at each other and then we looked away quick because we were afraid we'd burst out laughing and get in trouble with Miss Valentine. In the end we had to cover our mouths with our hands so nobody would hear us giggling.

Afterwards the teacher said it was very romantic, but all the way home, you and I laughed out loud and took turns imitating the king saying "lahv." We wondered if that was how people in England say "love."

And when we got to your house, your mother said it was a disgusting sin because the woman he loved—or lahved—was divorced, and not once but twice! A double disgusting sin, your mother said. My grandma and grandpa lived on Brookside Avenue that year too—remember?—and my grandpa told us the king was a dope.

And when he said that, you and I giggled all the rest of the day.

Well, I was just thinking, Aggie—I haven't got anybody to giggle with anymore. I miss that.

And this makes letter number eight and I haven't heard a peep out of you!

Love (or lahv),
Hannah

P.S. Hey, you know what that king who didn't want to be king's name was? *Edward!* The same as that boy from Kansas who wrote, *I haven't got a mountain. I have a cow.* I wonder if all Edwards are dopes.

November 12, 1937

Dear Hannah,

1. maraschino cherries
2. maraschino cherries
3. maraschino cherries
4. maraschino cherries
5. maraschino cherries

Sentence: *Maraschino cherries* are in a jar on the counter at Singer's Candy Store on Freeman Street in the Bronx, New York. Every sundae has one on the top. Charlotte russes from Beck's Bakery on the corner also have a *maraschino cherry* on the top. Hannah saves the *maraschino cherry* for last.

Love,
Grandma

P.S. Here is homework for *you,* teacher. Draw me a picture of a charlotte russe.

November 15, 1937

Dear President Roosevelt,

We listened to you on the radio last night. You forgot to say "My friends"! I held my breath so long I nearly exploded!

Love from your friend anyway,
Hannah

November 20, 1937

Dear Grandma,

Here is the homework you asked me to draw, only instead of drawing one charlotte russe, I drew two. (The second one I traced after I made the first one.) Here's why:

After you eat the whipped cream off the top of a charlotte russe and get down to the cake which you think is going to be big, all you really get is about two bites! The cake is so very delicious that after I eat the cherry, which I save for last, and lick the whipped cream off my fingers, I always wish I had more. So instead of drawing just one charlotte russe, I drew two. That way a person could get twice as much cake. Do you think it's a good picture?

Love to you and Grandpa,
Hannah

November 25, 1937

Dear Hannah,

Yes, I do think you made good pictures of the charlotte russe. But I never knew there was such a small piece of cake inside. Grandpa said next time he'll buy you two. He liked your drawings so much he took them to Beck's Bakery to show them.

Beck's liked the drawings so much they had them blown up and put in their window.

We can't wait to see you.

Love from Grandpa and me,
Grandma

P.S. Too bad you couldn't come this week. Fred Astaire and Ginger Rogers are playing at the movies one night and Shirley Temple the other.

December 1, 1937

Dear Grandma,

My dance teacher, Miss Dobbin, gives me a pain! Just when I thought I was coming for Christmas vacation so I could stay with you and Grandpa a long time, guess what happened! She's making us have dance recitals! Two performances, both over vacation. Sunday, December 19, and Sunday, December 26. And every day in between, we have to have rehearsals! I'm really mad. I like to tap-dance but not better than coming to the candy store.

I told Ma I don't want to be in the recital if I have to miss my visit and guess what she said: at fifty cents a lesson we won't be getting our money's worth if I don't dance!

Why didn't Miss Dobbin tell us sooner? Then I would have come for Thanksgiving vacation and at least we would have had four days. We could have seen Fred Astaire and Ginger Rogers and Shirley Temple too. Now I'll have to wait till Christmas vacation is over, and it will have to be only for a weekend again. It's not fair.

I'm mad at Miss Dobbin.

Love to you and Grandpa,
Hannah

P.S. How do you blow up a charlotte russe?

And another thing about Miss Dobbin: She picked me to dance in "Alexander's Ragtime Band." I wanted to do "On the Good Ship Lollipop." She never gives you what you want.

December 7, 1937

Dear Hannah,

Whenever you come, you'll come and we'll be happy. And as for your Miss Dobbin, maybe *she* never gives you what you want, but at your Grandma and Grandpa Singer's candy store, we will always give you what you want. You can tap-dance "Alexander's Ragtime Band" *and* "On the Good Ship Lollipop" for us too. You know what we always tell everybody? We have a granddaughter who can tap-dance better than Shirley Temple. Grandpa says to tell you he wishes we could see you in those recitals.

Love from

Grandma who-can't-wait-to-see-you-whenever

P.S. Beck's Bakery has a son who is a photographer. He blows up a picture with a thing called an enlarger. It makes it look bigger.

December 9, 1937

My dear niece Hannah,

Hello from your aunt Becky who you didn't hear from in a long time!

Don't think I forgot you, but my dear teeny little thoroughbred dog Poopala-darling is not in the best of health and I have been busy caring for her. She has to have shots.

Since winter is upon us I just finished knitting her a little pink wool jacket so she shouldn't get pneumonia on her daily constitutional.

Now I thought I would knit another jacket for your big jumping mutt, Skippy. You know mutts are not my type but since you are my favorite person in the world I am making an exception.

All you have to do is measure from the end of his neck to the beginning of his tail and also around his middle with a tape measure.

Usually I knit you guess-whats, as I know surprises are more fun, but since I had to ask you the measurements I can't surprise you this time.

Hoping you are all well, and waiting to get the measurements, I send you love and kisses,

Aunt Becky

P.S. I will make Skippy's jacket red-and-white candy stripes to match the stocking cap I made you last year that your mother said you liked so much.

December 12, 1937

Dear Aggie,

I'm sorry you can't be here for Miss Dobbin's dance recital this year. I know you thought the recitals were kind of boring because you had to watch all that sappy ballet and toe-dancing before the good stuff: *tap*, but you said it was worth it because of what came after: those big punch bowls filled with ginger ale and orange sherbet floating around in the middle and you can drink as many cups as you want. You and I always drank a *lot*. It won't be as much fun having punch without you there, Aggie. I think I'll just have one cup and go home.

Besides, I'm mad at Miss Dobbin because she picked a terrible time to have the recital this year: right over Christmas vacation, just when I wanted to go visit my grandma and grandpa at the candy store.

Love,
Hannah

P.S. Hey, Aggie, remember my aunt Becky who gave us autograph books last year and then knitted those itchy bumpy jackets to cover them up? Well, she's knitting a jacket for Skippy! I'll bet he'll get wild if we try to put it on him. He *hates* anything itchy.

This is my ninth letter.

December 14, 1937

Dear Aunt Becky,

From the beginning of Skippy's neck to the beginning of his tail is 26 inches. Around his middle is 27 inches.

My mother said it's very nice of you to knit a jacket for Skippy. When it's finished I'll let you know what Skippy says.

Remember my best friend, Aggie Branagan, who lived on Brookside Avenue in Nyack near us before we bought the Grand View Restaurant? Remember you knitted us jackets for autograph books you got us and you wrote inside each book?

Well, Aggie moved to Haverstraw and promised to be my pen pal but so far I wrote her nine letters and she didn't answer.

I am very disappointed in Aggie Branagan.

Love,
Hannah

December 18, 1937

Dear Grandma,

My mother says don't come to Miss Dobbin's recital. She says it's not worth it. She says Miss Dobbin is not that good of a teacher and the girls are kind of clumsy (except me) and it goes on forever. My father doesn't even come because the fathers have to wear suits and ties and he hates a suit and a tie.

Tell Grandpa not to feel bad—I'll dance the whole recital for both of you when I see you. My mother said it will be a command performance, like for the king of England.

Love,
Hannah

P.S. The only good thing at the recital is the ginger ale punch with orange sherbet in it. But it isn't as good as a chocolate egg cream you and Grandpa make for me.

Guess what? It's snowing! I *love* snow.

December 22, 1937

Dear Hannah,

Okay—we'll wait till you come and have the command performance here like the king of England. Grandpa says he's glad it's the king they have *now*, the one with the wife who wears blue dresses and hats with feathers to match and the two little girls, not that other king, who was a dope.

Love,
Grandma

P.S. It snowed here too. I don't love snow as much as you because we have to shovel the sidewalk in front of the store.

THE WHITE HOUSE
1600 Pennsylvania Avenue
Washington, D.C.

January 2, 1938

My dear friend Hannah Diamond,

Thank you for your letters of October 7 and 10 and for confiding your problems to me. It is most gratifying to me to hear from the people--especially young people.

I am very sorry about your friend. While I do not know at this moment of any young girl looking for a pen pal, should I meet up with one in the near future, rest assured I will pass on your name and address. In the meantime, be of good cheer! I am an optimist and always feel that everything will turn out all right in the end, both for our country and for our personal problems as well. Never give up!

You asked if I have a hobby. Enclosed is a small offering from my stamp collection. As president, I work all day ''trying to fix the hard times'' as you aptly put it. In the evening, I relax in my study, where I am writing to you from now, with my stamp collection and with my mail. This particular stamp, as you can see, is from Australia. I thought you might like the kangaroo.

Now, in answer to your question, Do I like hamburgers? Does Popeye's friend Wimpy like hamburgers? That's how much I like hamburgers!

I wish the Grand View Restaurant were just around the corner from the White House, for then I would come and order a hamburger with everything on top and with French fries too! I would have only one request: that the meat be rare--very rare. Our cook tends to make meat very well done, which is not to my taste, but she is convinced she knows more about what is good for me than I do.

Just reading your description of the hamburgers at the Grand View Restaurant makes me hungry. It might be of interest to you to know that President Theodore Roosevelt, who was my wife Eleanor Roosevelt's uncle, said business should give the people a square deal. So not only would he have approved of the hamburgers with four extra bites at the Grand View Restaurant--he probably would have claimed credit for THE SQUARE DEAL on your father's sign as well.

Thank you for thinking of me, my dear, for everyone likes to have friends, even a president.

I wish you and your family a happy new year--1938!

Sincerely, your friend,

Franklin Delano Roosevelt

Franklin Delano Roosevelt

FDR:MAL

January 5, 1938

Dear President Roosevelt,

I can't believe I've written to Aggie Branagan nine times and haven't received an answer and I wrote to the president of the United States four times and I did! (I wrote two other letters too but I guess you didn't get to read those yet.) My father said he read in the papers that you receive one thousand letters a day. It must take a long time to read a thousand letters a day and fix the hard times besides.

I don't know who was more excited, me or Mr. Powell. Mr. Powell is our mailman. He's from Iowa. Twice a day when he brings the mail he sits down and has a cup of coffee and tells us how much he misses Iowa. Today he played a trick on me.

He knows I'm waiting for a letter from Aggie. So every day he says to me, "No letter today, Hannah." Today he said, "There *is* a letter for you today, Hannah, but it's not from Aggie so I hope you won't be disappointed. It's from . . . *The president of the United States!*"

My mother ran over to see. My father ran over to see. Even Skippy ran over to see!

"Open it!" everybody said (except Skippy).

I ripped open the envelope.

The first thing I saw inside the letter was the stamp. I knew you would have a hobby, President Roosevelt!

I ran into my room and read your letter to myself first. It was so nice I ran back out and read it to my mother, my father, Skippy, and Mr. Powell.

My father liked what you said about the square hamburgers and President Theodore Roosevelt. My mother liked the whole letter except one thing: that you like hamburgers *rare*—very rare—and not well done like your cook makes everything.

My father said to my mother, "Aha! You see—even President Roosevelt likes meat to be rare." My mother likes meat well done, like your cook. She thinks it's healthier. My mother makes meat so well done, my father calls it shoe leather. My father and I think that's funny but my mother doesn't. She said she hopes *Mrs.* Roosevelt likes it well done like she does and like your cook does. My father said the cook should make it the way the president likes it. I was glad they didn't get in an argument over it the way they do at the supper table every night. Now, since your letter came, my father decided he's the winner of that argument.

Back to the stamp from Australia. That was really a coincidence because today I won a spelling bee in school and *Australia* was one of the words! We had to spell ten hard names of countries of the world: Abyssinia, Afghanistan, Australia, Czechoslovakia, Liberia, Lithuania, Mozambique, Romania, Tanganyika, and Yugoslavia. I was the only one who got them all right. I'm the best speller in my class. I never missed a word yet! (It's a good thing they don't have arithmetic bees, though. I'd get the booby prize.)

And then I came home and got the letter from you with the stamp from Australia inside. Don't you think that's a coincidence?

Mr. Powell was so excited he had two cups of coffee in a row and never even mentioned Iowa once!

Well, I have to go now, President Roosevelt. I have to

write to Aggie Branagan and tell her you wrote me a letter. Maybe then *she* will!

Thanks again for the stamp. I really like kangaroos. I'm glad you like hamburgers.

Love from your friend,
Hannah

P.S. After Mr. Powell left, my mother called up my grandma and grandpa in the Bronx, New York, and I read them your whole letter on the telephone. My grandfather said you should come to their candy store and he'll make you the biggest banana split in New York City. I'm going to see them soon. I can't wait!

January 10, 1938

Dear Aggie,

Guess what! You'll never guess in a million years so I'll tell you: *I got a letter from President Roosevelt!* He answered me after just two letters! So maybe now *you* would answer, since this is letter number ten.

Now another guess-what, but it's really a guess-where. Guess where I'm writing to you from: I'm on the bus going to New York City. I'm going to visit my grandmother and grandfather at their candy store in the Bronx! I'm bringing President Roosevelt's letter to show them, even though I already read it to them on the telephone, because I want them to see it in person. Also I want to show them what he put inside the envelope.

If you answer this letter, I'll tell you everything President Roosevelt said. And I'll tell you what he sent me. But only if you write.

Love,
Hannah

P.S. I read this over and it sounds like I was trying to bribe you. I know that's against the law because I once heard somebody say so on the radio. I think it was the Lone Ranger. Also it isn't nice. So I *will* tell you about the letter and what was inside, but later, not now. Because now something is itching me. I think there's a mosquito on this bus. I don't hear it but I feel itchy and that's usually from mosquito bites. I started to scratch but the lady in the next seat looked at me so I stopped. My mother always says if you scratch, people might think you have bugs!

TO BE CONTINUED

Hannah

Still January 10, 1938

Dear Aggie,

Here I am at the candy store. (And still itching.)

And here's the second half of the letter I wrote the first half of on the bus:

What President Roosevelt said was if he ever meets a girl who wants a pen pal he'll give her my name. (I wish it would be you!) He said never give up! And he said he wishes he could have a rare hamburger from the Grand View Restaurant and what he sent inside the envelope was a stamp with a kangaroo on it.

There, I kept my promise to tell you. We always said people should keep their promises—right, Aggie?

My grandpa met the bus at the George Washington Bridge and we rode on a lot of subways. As soon as we got here, my grandma made me a chocolate egg cream. That's like an ice cream soda without the ice cream. I don't know why they call it an egg cream—it doesn't have any eggs. But it's delicious.

Now Grandma's in the back of the store making supper and Grandpa is up in their apartment taking a nap. After supper Grandma and I are going to see *Snow White and the Seven Dwarfs* at the movies. Remember how we loved cartoons? *Snow White* is like a cartoon but it's as long as a whole movie. I can't wait to see it. And tomorrow there's a movie with the Dionne quintuplets!

My grandma and I love the movies. We always go when I come to visit. We go to Loew's Freeman Street where they give free dishes. And on the way back Grandma always imitates the actors and actresses and makes me laugh. (Last time I was here we saw a movie with Maurice Chevalier and he sang a song called "Mimi." On the way home, Grandma sang "Mimi" in the street! She tried to imitate Maurice Chevalier's French accent and it was funny because Grandma has a Jewish accent.) And after we get back to the store Grandpa always makes us an ice cream soda.

I love to come here. I wish I could stay forever.

My favorite customer just came in. His name is Jims. He's a regular customer—this is a neighborhood candy store, and I know all the "regulars."

I'll just stop a minute to wait on him and then I'll finish writing.

Jims had a two-cents plain. That's a little glass of seltzer. He always has the same. I don't like it—it's just water with bubbles. I like chocolate egg creams.

I showed him President Roosevelt's letter, which I brought to show my grandma and grandpa, and he got all excited. He said he likes President Roosevelt too and has something he wants to ask him but he hasn't got good handwriting like mine. He asked me if I would be his secretary and write it for him.

My grandma heard him from the back of the store. She said, "Stop teasing Hannah, Jims!"

Jims said, "I'm not teasing, Moms—I really mean it." Jims calls my grandma and grandpa Moms and Pops and he calls himself Jims. I asked him why he doesn't call me Hannahs. He said I don't look like a Hannahs. I asked him if President Roosevelt looks like a President Roosevelts. He said he looks like an FDR.

I said I know how to write a letter like a secretary. I see secretaries in the movies. The boss says, "Take a letter." The secretary writes it down.

So Jims said, "Take a letter," and I wrote it down even though my grandma thought I shouldn't.

Jims just went out to mail the letter on his way to work. I wrote it for him with a pen. But first I wrote it in pencil and then I copied it over. He said I could keep the pencil copy. Maybe you would like to hear what I wrote when I was pretending to be his secretary, Aggie. I'll copy my pencil copy for you. Here's what he said:

> Dear FDR,
>
> I am a poor working man who works the night shift at the DuRite Laundry in the Bronx, New York.
>
> My boss doesn't pay me enough and if I ask for a raise he says I'm lucky I have a job at all in these hard times and I shouldn't complain or I might get fired!
>
> My girlfriend works in DuRite too. I would like to take her out on a date to the movies and for an ice cream soda or a sundae after, but on my low salary I can't afford it. All I can afford is a two-cents plain.
>
> I just found out my *boss* asked my girlfriend out on a date for next Saturday night! He said he'd take her to the movies and then out *dancing* and then for an ice cream soda or a sundae. She didn't say yes but she didn't say no either. She said she'd think it over.

> I'm worried if she goes, maybe he'll ask her to marry him and then she won't be my girlfriend anymore. But if I complain maybe he'll fire me.
>
> Everybody says President Roosevelt is the working man's friend. So, FDR, could you lend me five bucks before Saturday night so I can take my girlfriend out on a date and she won't marry the boss?

And he signed it *James Thomas.*

Grandma said again, "Will you stop teasing that girl?" but Jims said he was going right out and mail the letter on his way to work.

I told Grandma I thought a mosquito followed me from the bus to the subway to the candy store because I got itchy again, but she said the same thing my mother always does: "Don't scratch."

Well, Aggie, I have to eat supper and go to the movies now.

I won't call this letter number eleven, because it's still the same one continued from the bus, which was number ten. See, I'm trying to be fair.

I hope President Roosevelt lends Jims the five bucks, don't you?

Love,
Hannah

January 11

P.S. In bed I itched all night and in the morning I told Grandma the mosquito must have followed me even to the movies and she looked at me and said, "You've got more than mosquito bites—you've got a *rash*." And she called her doctor, Dr. Bernard, and you know what he said? He said I've got measles, Aggie!

Measles!

January 12, 1938

To Miss Hopkins
Liberty Street School
Nyack, New York

Dear Miss Hopkins,

I'm sorry I'll be out of school for a while. I came to the Bronx, New York, to visit my grandparents and I got the measles! Dr. Bernard, my grandma's doctor, was surprised. He said he hasn't seen any cases of measles in the Bronx lately.

I'm writing to you because I thought maybe you could send me some homework, c/o Mr. and Mrs. Marcus Singer, 3451 Freeman Street, Bronx, New York. In the meantime, I am playing school with my grandma.

Love,
Hannah

P.S. I have to stay in a dim room and measles are very itchy but I'm trying not to scratch because Dr. Bernard said it could make trouble. Also he gives *prizes* from his little black bag when he comes to see you if you don't scratch. The prizes are mostly rings—like the pretty ones in Cracker Jack boxes. He lets you pick your own colors. So far I have a red and a pink.

January 12, 1938

Dear Hannah,

Hello from your neighbor Mrs. Warner!

I was sorry to hear that you have the measles.

I am sending you some of my cookies that you like to have with Postum when we listen to *The Witch's Tale* at my house. Please give some to your grandma and grandpa too and tell them hello from your neighbor who likes your grandma's fluffy matzo balls.

Get well quick. Don't scratch.

Love,
Mrs. Warner

January 13, 1938

Dear Mrs. Warner,

Thanks for the get-well letter and the delicious cookies.

We listen to all the radio programs, except *The Witch's Tale* of course. And my grandma even got Postum for me to drink like you and I do at your house. So except for the itching, it's fun to listen to the radio and eat cookies and drink Postum with your grandma and grandpa.

I don't scratch, even though it's hard not to, because Dr. Bernard gives rings if you control yourself. So far I have pink, red, purple, and green.

Love,
Hannah

P.S. Grandma thought it was so nice of you to send the cookies—she says next time she comes to visit us she'll bring you a whole jar of chicken soup with matzo balls. She says you appreciate her fluffy matzo balls lots more than I do. I like only matzo balls that are hard as rocks, the way my aunt Becky (the bad knitter) makes them. Grandma says matzo balls are not supposed to be hard as rocks, but I like things that go crunch.

January 14, 1938

Miss Hannah Diamond
c/o Mr. and Mrs. Marcus Singer
3451 Freeman Street
Bronx, New York

Dear Hannah,

I am so sorry you have the measles. Tell your grandma's doctor that if he came to Nyack, he would see many cases of measles. Suddenly half the class has them!

Enclosed are get-well cards from the half of the class who are still here.

Also enclosed along with the get-well cards is a letter that came for you yesterday in care of our class. I see it is postmarked Wichita, Kansas. This tells me that you wrote to the boy whose name you picked from the pen pal box even though you really wanted a girl. You are a good sport, Hannah! When you get back home, you may read the letter to the class!

Your teacher,
Dorothy Hopkins

P.S. Playing school with your grandma will suffice as homework till you get back.

January 9, 1938

Dear Hannah,

My teacher that made me put my name on that piece of paper thinks I didn't answer the letter you wrote me.

I told her I did answer but you didn't answer my answer.

She doesn't believe me. She says I have to have a letter to show her to prove I answered.

So answer or I'll get zero in being a pen pal.

Edward Winchley

January 15, 1938

Dear Aggie,

I am itching so much I can't stand it. But I don't scratch because I want rings.

I made up a club for me to join. It's called the IAITD Club. I'm the only member so I'm the president.

You are lucky you don't have measles, Aggie because besides the itching, my eyes hurt. This is my eleventh letter.

In case you are wondering, IAITD stands for I Am Itching To Death.

Love,
Hannah

P.S. Guess what? That dumb boy from Kansas I got out of the pen pal box on Miss Hopkins's desk—the one who wrote me that smart aleck letter: *I haven't got a mountain. I have a cow*—wrote to me again! He sent it to school! Miss Hopkins sent it to me here, so now I have to answer it or his teacher will give him a zero in being a pen pal. (His teacher sounds even dumber than he does.) Well, I'll answer him all right—one answer for the teacher and another one for him—but he won't like it.

January 16, 1938

Dear Edward,

Thank you very much for your answer to my letter.

I am sorry to hear that you don't have a mountain. Mountains are very interesting.

I am glad to hear you have a cow. Cows must be very interesting too.

Your friend,
Hannah

January 16, 1938

Dear Edward,

There—now you have a letter to show your teacher. But *this* letter is just for you.

The reason I didn't answer your letter, Edward, is, you call that a letter?

To tell you the truth, I think you *deserve* a zero in being a pen pal. If you want to know, I didn't really want to write to you either. I wanted a girl, like my friend Aggie who moved and doesn't answer me. But my teacher said if I didn't write to you I wouldn't be a good sport. So I wrote to you. I wrote you three long pages. You wrote me two lines. Do you think two lines deserve an answer? I don't. So I didn't.

So now you have a letter to show your teacher because I wouldn't want anybody to get zero in anything because of me even if they deserve it. I am very crabby because I have the measles and I can't scratch or I won't get a ring from the doctor.

Your friend,
Hannah

P.S. Why did you write to me at my school? Now my teacher says I have to read your letter to the class when I get back. I'll have to read it standing up, which I hate. I like to read sitting down.

January 18, 1938

Miss Hannah Diamond
c/o Mr. and Mrs. Marcus Singer
3451 Freeman Street
Bronx, New York

Dear Hannah,

Thank you very much for the homework that you made up for yourself and sent to me. You got 100.

I am glad to hear from your mother that you are beginning to feel a little better. I hope you have won many rings from the doctor.

You will be surprised to hear that I too now have the measles!

I hope to be back in school in time for your return.

I also hope you enjoyed the get-well cards from your classmates and the letter from your nice new pen pal in Wichita, Kansas.

Your teacher,
Dorothy Hopkins

Hannah Diamond
Route 9W
Grand View, New York

President Roosevelt's Secretary MAL
The White House
1600 Pennsylvania Avenue
Washington, D. C.

January 21, 1938

Dear Miss MAL,

I am Hannah Diamond, the girl who wrote letters to President Roosevelt from the Grand View Restaurant with the square hamburgers and he sent me that nice answer and a stamp with a kangaroo.

My mother and father just came to the Bronx, New York, to bring me back home from having the measles while visiting my grandparents at their candy store.

The first night I was there, one of the customers asked me to be his secretary and write a letter to President Roosevelt for him. Did you get it? My mother says secretaries read the mail first. It was signed *James Thomas* (but I call him Jims). He asked President Roosevelt to lend him five bucks so he could take his girlfriend out on a date so she wouldn't go out with their boss from DuRite

Laundry who is mean and doesn't pay Jims enough money.

I wrote the letter in pencil first and then copied it over in ink. Jims said I could keep the pencil copy. I just showed it to my mother and she says I shouldn't have written it. She says I owe President Roosevelt an apology. But when I sat down at my desk to write she said I shouldn't pester the president. I said, "Then how can I apologize?" She said, "Write to his secretary." I said, "Who's his secretary?"

She showed me on the bottom of the letter he wrote me, on the left-hand side: FDR:MAL. MAL, she said, is the secretary. My mother used to be a bookkeeper in an office before she got married so she knows about things like that.

I said, "What am I apologizing *for*?" She said, "Two things. The first is that it isn't nice to ask for money." I told her Jims only asked President Roosevelt to *lend* him the money. She said he already owes Grandma and Grandpa for about fifty two-cents plains. I said he'll pay them back but she said I still shouldn't have written the letter for him. And the second thing she said I should apologize for was for saying "five bucks." She said that's slang and a person should not use slang to a president. I didn't know "five bucks" was slang. My teacher always tells us not to use slang too.

My teacher is Miss Hopkins. She got measles, just like me and half the class.

Now we're all back in school.

So would you tell President Roosevelt that Hannah Diamond from the Grand View Restaurant says hello and she's sorry she tried to be a secretary and wrote a letter for somebody that her mother says she shouldn't have written? And she's sorry she used slang but she didn't know it was slang.

My friend Aggie Branagan who moved and was supposed to be my pen pal still didn't write to me even though I wrote to her eleven times already.

Your friend,
Hannah Diamond

P.S. How did you get to be a secretary?

Hannah Diamond
Route 9W
Grand View, New York

UNITED STATES POSTAGE
3 CENTS 3

Mr. James Thomas
℅ Mr. and Mrs. Marcus Singer
3451 Freeman Street
Bronx, New York

January 22, 1938

Dear Jims,

Did he send you the five bucks?

Love,
Hannah

January 23, 1938

Dear Grandma,

Ma told me to write you and Grandpa a thank-you note for being so nice to me when I had measles. She didn't have to tell me that—I was going to write you a thank-you note as soon as I got home.

But first she wanted me to write an apology to President Roosevelt for writing the letter from Jims. She thought I shouldn't have written it too, like you. She said it isn't nice to ask for money from anybody but especially the president. I said Jims just asked for a *loan*. She said he owes you for fifty two-cents plains already. He'll pay you back, Grandma—I know he will. Jims is nice—I like him because he's friendly. And I'm sorry because he's so poor.

What Ma doesn't know is I'm going to write *you* an apology too and I have an extra thank-you for you for not telling her what it is I have to apologize *for*. You said it's just between you and me. Oh, grandmas are wonderful!

Whenever I come to visit you and Grandpa in the Bronx, I always wish I could stay longer. This time I got my wish, except for the itching. You made having measles almost be fun!

I loved the way whenever one of you went down from the apartment to the candy store, the other came up, always with a surprise: Crayolas, a sketch pad, a watercolor box with a brush, colored pencils, colored paper, scissors, paste, clay, movie magazines, comic books—everything! And all those different flavors of ice cream—eleven! (Here at the Grand View Restaurant, we have just chocolate, vanilla, and strawberry.) I'm still trying to decide which was my favorite. I think the maple walnut.

Please thank Grandpa for bringing the radio into the bedroom while I was there and for listening to all my favorite programs with me: *Let's Pretend; The Singing Lady; Little Orphan Annie; Jack Armstrong, the All-American Boy; Jack Benny; Burns and Allen; The Lone Ranger;* and best of all, *The Goldbergs.* I love when Molly Goldberg says, "Yoo-hoo, Mrs. Bloom!"

And please thank Dr. Bernard for all the rings. I'm wearing one on every finger right this minute.

But what I really want to thank you for the most, Grandma, is the thing Ma doesn't know about, thanks to you for not telling.

About the broken little orange teacup.

I know you told me I don't have to apologize, but I *want* to. And what I want to apologize for is more than even the teacup, which I know was a wedding present and that's why you kept it with all those other pretty things behind the glass doors in your china cabinet that you call your *chinik.* I know they're just to look at, not to use, and that's why you keep the doors locked with that little key.

So my biggest apology is for this: that I pestered you again—like that time at the carnival with Aggie and her father and the hot dogs and the beer. If I hadn't pestered you to open your *chinik* door with the key, the little orange teacup would still be there, standing in a row with the five other ones just like it on the shelf.

Ma always tells me, "Hannah, don't pester!" and I always

promise not to—I *mean* not to, Grandma—but then I always do.

When I saw that shiny little orange teacup with the golden rim standing there in a row with the others (right under the shelf with that pitcher that looks like a pineapple), I couldn't resist. I said to myself, *If I could just have a cup of Postum in one of those pretty little orange teacups, I feel like I wouldn't itch so much.* I never saw you open that door with the little key before. I was holding my breath. I should have listened when you said you don't use those things because they could break. I should have listened when you said, "Don't drop it!" I was so sure I wouldn't drop it. But then when I tried to hold my pinky up in the air like fancy ladies in the movies when they hold a cup, my hand lost its balance and I dropped it.

I know you said later I shouldn't cry over spilled Postum. But it wasn't the Postum I cried about. And it was very nice of you to go out and buy me two charlotte russes to cheer me up afterward. Even Dr. Bernard gave me an extra ring that day, remember? But if I had listened to Ma saying (in my head), "Hannah, don't pester!" it wouldn't have happened in the first place. So I *do* apologize (my second apology this week) and I thank you again, Grandma, for not saying anything to anybody about it—not even Grandpa! And for saying it's just between you and me.

You are the nicest grandma in the whole world.

Love,
Hannah

P.S. I forgot to thank you also for playing school and asking for one hard word each day. I kept a list of all the ones you learned: *cough, laugh, rough, tough, knife, knock, knickers,* and *knuckles.* You learned every one, and all of them are harder than *comb.* It's fun being the teacher when you're the pupil!

January 26, 1938

Dear Teacher Hannah,

Thank you for teaching me all the new hard words.

But thank you for teaching me an even more important lesson. Pretty things should be enjoyed, not hidden behind locked doors. Who wants to live in a museum? Using things is better than just looking at them!

And if you say to a child, "Don't drop it!" the child is going to drop it. Pinkies in the air have nothing to do with it.

So next time you come, Hannah, we'll have a tea party (or a Postum party like that neighbor of yours). I'll let you open the glass doors with the key. We'll *both* have Postum from the little orange teacups. And charlotte russes too.

Grandchildren are more important than cups!

Besides, how many cups does a person need?

Love from your favorite pupil,

Grandma

January 27, 1938

Dear Aggie,

I'm back home. The measles are gone and I'm still waiting for a letter from you. Or else a new friend. Remember Bunny Hunnicutt? She says she's starting a club, the GWMDTOGTAMN Club, and I might be invited to be a member. It's a secret club and I'm not allowed to tell about it. Maybe Bunny Hunnicutt could be my new friend.

But I'd rather have you. So if you would write and be my pen pal, then you would still be my friend and I wouldn't *need* a new one. A letter is like talking to somebody; that's why a pen pal is like a friend. You *talk* to your friends. I *need* a pen pal—a real one—not like that smart aleck Edward Winchley from Wichita, Kansas. I hope I never hear from him again. Because even if I do, I am not going to answer him.

Have you got a new best friend in Haverstraw? I know it would be polite of me to say I hope you do. But I guess I'm not polite because I hope you don't.

Love,
Hannah

P.S. This is my twelfth letter. Did you see *Snow White and the Seven Dwarfs*? It was *wonderful!*

January 30, 1938

My dear niece Hannah,

Enclosed is Skippy's jacket—finally. May he wear it in good health. With all this cold weather and so much snow, it's just in time.

I was very sorry to hear what happened to you in the Bronx. I would have come from Brooklyn on the subway to pay you a sick call, but I never had measles myself and was afraid I could get it and pass it on to my sweet little thoroughbred doggy, Poopala-darling. As you know, she has a heart condition and is very delicate.

I was also sorry to hear that you and your grandma missed the movie *The Dionne Quintuplets*. I know how you love the Dionne quintuplets, but don't feel bad. I myself saw the movie last week so next time I see you I'll tell you the whole story. Aunt Becky to the rescue!

Remember how I told you the whole story of the opera *Madame Butterfly* last year when I visited and you and your best friend took your dog, Skippy, to the dog show at the movies so you missed the whole Metropolitan Opera broadcast on the radio? Your father and I listened together and when Skippy was thrown out of the theater for behaving like a hooligan and you came home, I told you and your friend the whole story that you missed—remember? Well, next time I see you I'll fill you in on *The Dionne Quintuplets* in the same way.

Now, good news! I found a perfect present to make up for missing the movie. It will take a while to send because I have to knit some guess-whats to go with it.

You will love this present so much, when you see it you'll faint.

Love and kisses,
Aunt Becky

THE WHITE HOUSE
1600 Pennsylvania Avenue
Washington, D.C.

January 28, 1938

My dear friend Hannah,

I have now had time to take a poll among all my friends and staff and I find that you are the only person I know who stands up in bed for ''The Star Spangled Banner.''

Therefore your teacher is right: You probably are the most patriotic person in the whole United States.

With devotion like this, how can our country fail?

Enclosed is another stamp from one of the ten countries with the hard names on your spelling bee: Tanganyika. You can see from the head and the beginning of the neck (though the rest of it has to be imagined) that this one is a giraffe. I hope it meets with your approval.

Keep on being patriotic, my dear, and keep on never missing a word in spelling.

Best wishes from your friend,

Franklin Delano Roosevelt

P.S. On checking my radio address of November 14, I find that you are absolutely right: I did forget to say ''my friends''! I truly regret being the cause of your holding your breath for so long that you nearly exploded! I should have been born an elephant, for an elephant never forgets! To make amends, enclosed find an extra stamp of an elephant from Liberia.

FDR:MAL

February 1, 1938

Dear Grandma,

President Roosevelt called me "my dear" again! And he said I'm patriotic!

Did I tell you that Aunt Becky knitted a jacket for Skippy? Did he get mad when Ma put it on him! He looked like this:

He rolled around and jumped up in the air and barked so much we had to take it off him. Then he growled at it like it was alive and he grabbed it with his teeth and before we could stop him, he chewed it all to pieces! My father and I couldn't stop laughing but my mother said we should be ashamed of ourselves because Aunt Becky had worked hard knitting all those stripes. And she said, "Now, who is going to write Becky a thank-you note?" My father said Skippy should write his own thank-you note, which I thought was funny but my mother didn't. So in the end my father went out to his "office" in the garage and said he had to write a letter to the editor and as usual I am stuck writing the thank-you note.

Love to you and Grandpa,
Hannah

P.S. What I can't understand is why my mother hates the lumps of paste Aggie Branagan's father left under the roses on the wallpaper in my bedroom but she doesn't mind the lumps in Aunt Becky's knitting.

February 1, 1938

Dear Aunt Becky,

Thanks for the letter and Skippy's candy-striped jacket. I put it on him and he got very frisky. He rolled around and barked and jumped up in the air. And I think he thought it really *was* a candy cane because he tried to eat it.

I'm glad you saw *The Dionne Quintuplets.* I thought maybe I could see it at the Nyack movies after I came home, but my mother said it already played here while I was having measles in the Bronx. So now I know I'll still get to hear the whole story from you—someday. No hurry, Aunt Becky.

About finding me a present to make up for missing the movie, that was very nice of you. My mother said it'll be a consolation prize. But you don't have to bother knitting me any clothes because I already have so many clothes you knitted me. I have sweaters, jackets, scarves, and mittens. I even still have the red-and-white stocking cap that matches Skippy's jacket and that I wore up to the top of the mountain the time we had the big snow. And when my one galosh came off and I couldn't find it under the snow, I walked down the mountain with your stocking cap on my *foot.*

One thing about your knitting, Aunt Becky, it never wears out, so you see, you don't really have to knit me anything new.

Did I tell you that my friend Aggie, who you remember from last year, moved and we were supposed to be pen pals but so far I wrote her twelve letters and didn't get an answer?

Love,
Hannah

February 3, 1938

Dear Aggie,

I got two letters this week, a wonderful one and a terrible one.

The wonderful one was from President Roosevelt (again!). He said I'm probably the most patriotic person in the whole United States! And he sent me a stamp from Tanganyika with a giraffe's head and the top of the neck. The last time he wrote to me he sent me a stamp from Liberia with an elephant because an elephant never forgets. I love President Roosevelt.

The terrible letter was from my aunt Becky from Brooklyn. You remember Aunt Becky—she's the one who made us listen to the whole story of that opera *Madame Butterfly* last year the day we took Skippy to the dog show and he lost. (After you went home, she made me listen to her *sing* the whole story of *Madame Butterfly*. I don't even like operas to begin with—my *father* does—and Aunt Becky has a terrible voice but she thinks it's good so I had to listen.)

Also, she said she's *knitting* me something new—HELP! Remember, she sent you and me each a present after she was here, an autograph book with a knitted jacket? Your jacket was blue and mine was red, but the books were the same and she wrote on the first page of mine, *To my dear niece Hannah, my favorite person in the world, Aunt Becky,* and on the first page of yours, *To my dear niece Hannah's best friend.* (*Am* I still your best friend, Aggie? You're still mine.) And both jackets were itchy, lumpy, and bumpy, like all of Aunt Becky's knitting, but my mother always says it's not the present, it's the thought that counts. Aunt Becky knits jackets for *everything*—all my books, my father's cigar box, and my mother's flowerpots even. She knitted Skippy a jacket and he *hated* it. He chewed it all up. I'm afraid to tell her about President Roosevelt and the stamps because I know she'll knit a tiny little jacket for the stamps and I don't want her to.

It's hard work being somebody's favorite person in the world.

I like Aunt Becky, except for her knitting and her singing, but I *hate* that bratty little yapping dog Poopaladarling. I like Skippy better, even if he's a mutt. He's a *friendly* mutt.

Love,
Hannah

P.S. This is my thirteenth letter.

February 5, 1938

Dear Hannah,

I am MAL, and your mother was right--I <u>am</u> President Roosevelt's secretary.

My full name is Marguerite Alice LeHand, but everybody calls me Missy.

I was very pleased to receive your letter of January 21. Let me assure you you have nothing to worry about because the letter you spoke of, from one James Thomas of the Bronx, New York, either got lost in the mails or else it was never actually mailed out, for we have no record of receiving such a letter. I have three assistants and we all looked into it. President Roosevelt receives many letters asking him for many things, but none of us recalls a recent request for ''five bucks'' to take a girlfriend out on a date and beat the boss to it.

Even if the letter had arrived, you needn't have worried about using the expression ''five bucks.'' It may be slang, but a great deal of slang is used nowadays and ''five bucks'' is fairly inoffensive.

When I was your age, I can remember my own mother telling us children not to use slang. My teacher too told us not to refer to other children as ''kids'' because that was slang and, as she constantly reminded us, ''A kid is a goat.''

I'm sorry to hear you had measles and glad to hear you are now back at school.

About your friend who moved and still hasn't answered your letters, I hope that eventually you will hear from her. I am still in touch with a friend who lived only a few houses away in Somerville, Massachusetts, where I grew up, and I know how sorry I would be to lose her—or any friend.

Of course my best friends these days are President and Mrs. Roosevelt. They are the kindest, most generous people I have ever met in my life and I value them above all others.

I can't think of a better person to lead us out of these hard times than Franklin Delano Roosevelt. I know from your past correspondence that you agree with me.

You asked how I became a secretary. Well, after high school, I went to secretarial school to learn all the skills. I did my best to master them and then I went to New York City to practice.

There I met Mr. and Mrs. Roosevelt (I say Mr. because he was not yet president—all of this was long before you were born—though he was already involved in politics. He was running for vice president. I'm sorry to say he lost.) At any rate, Mrs. Roosevelt was impressed with my work, thought I was efficient, and asked me to come to Hyde Park to help not-yet-President Roosevelt with his correspondence. I have been his secretary ever since. So I can really thank her for starting me on my way to the most rewarding job of my career.

Do you have ambitions to become a secretary when you grow up? I ask you this question since you say you already ''took a letter.'' If so, I would be glad to offer you tips on how to go about becoming a really crackerjack secretary.

Sincerely yours,

M. A. LeHand

Marguerite LeHand
(but call me Missy)

February 6, 1938

Dear Hannah,

I gave my teacher the letter that was for her and then she believed me that I wrote to you so I didn't get a zero. She said you were a little stiff, whatever that means. I don't ask her no questions.

If you wrote to me at my school I would like it fine. Then she would believe me better.

The letter that was for me I kept.

Why did you say I deserved a zero? What did you get so mad at me for? I didn't do nothing wrong.

And why did you say my first letter that the teacher made me write was not a letter? It was the first letter I ever wrote in my life. I didn't know two lines was not enough. Is this better?

Edward Winchley

P.S. I hope you got rid of those measles. And I hope there wasn't no germs in your letter.

February 10, 1938

Dear Edward,

Well, well, so your teacher thinks I'm a little stiff. Tell her I did it on purpose.

I hope you won't think I have bad manners, but I have to tell you something:

Your English, Edward, is terrible.

You wrote *three* double negatives. A double negative makes a positive. My teacher, Miss Hopkins, told us that.

For example, when you say, "I don't ask her no questions," it means you do ask her *some* questions. You should say, "I don't ask her *any* questions."

When you say, "I didn't do nothing wrong," it means you did do *something* wrong. You should say, "I didn't do *anything* wrong."

And when you say, "I hope there wasn't no germs in your letter," it means you hope there are *some* germs in my letter. You should say, "I hope there weren't *any* germs in your letter."

Since I might be a teacher when I grow up, I hope you won't mind my practicing on you.

I always play school with my grandma and she lets me be the teacher and give her hard spelling words.

And yes, your last letter was better than the first one. I'm sorry I yelled at you about that first one. How was I supposed to know it was the first letter you ever wrote in your life?

Your friend,
Hannah

P.S. But I really don't think it was very polite of you to wonder if I sent you *germs.* I never heard of a germ that traveled through the mail—especially all the way from New York State to Kansas.

February 14, 1938

Dear Hannah,

My teacher never told us nothing about double negatives and positives. I don't even know what that means. Guess what. I don't even want to know.

I don't like to play school. It's bad enough I have to *go* to school.

Please don't tell me I'm terrible in English.

My teacher already told me that. She also told me I'm terrible in writing too and even in talking. She says the rest of the class talks too much and I don't talk enough.

My father says I'm terrible at getting up at five o'clock in the morning to do the chores.

My mother tells me I'm terrible at keeping my room in order. She says it's like a pig's pen. We have a pig so I know that's an insult.

Even my little sister tells me I'm terrible at being a big brother. She wants me to read her stories. I don't like to read.

So please I can't stand no more people telling me what I'm terrible in.

I'm good in arithmetic. But nobody says nothing about that.

Edward Winchley

P.S. The only person who never tells me what I'm terrible in is our cow Mathilda. She is going to have a calf this spring. When I have to go out to milk her in the dark at five o'clock I talk to her softly and she looks at me with kind eyes. She is the only one who likes me in the world.

February 15, 1938

Dear President Roosevelt,

Thank you for the giraffe from Tanganyika and the elephant from Liberia. I put them next to the kangaroo from Australia inside a walnut shell in one of the cubbyholes in my rolltop desk. That's where I keep all my special things.

And now I have to tell you some bad news.

I missed a word in spelling.

Here it is: *restaurateur.*

Could you spell that?

I spelled it *restauranteur.* I still think that's how it should be spelled.

If only I didn't try to be fancy I'd still be the only one in the class who never had a wrong-spelled word.

What happened was we were supposed to fill in a blank and tell what our father does. Last year when we had to fill in the blank I wrote *proprietor of restaurant.* Lots of people spell *proprietor* wrong. They write *er* at the end instead of *or.* I don't.

But this year once I saw the word *restauranteur.* At least that's what I thought I saw. I thought it was a very fancy word.

So when we had to fill in the blank about what our father does, I wrote *restauranteur.* I thought my teacher would say, "Well done, Hannah!"

Instead she called me up to her desk and said, "This is spelled wrong, Hannah. It's *restaurateur.*"

I said, "My father owns a restaurant."

She said, "The word for that is *restaurateur.*"

I said, "But he owns a restaurant, not a restaurat."

She said, "But it's spelled *restaurateur.*"

I said to myself, "I should know. It's *my* father." But I didn't say it out loud. My mother says never talk fresh to a teacher.

So she changed it to *restaurateur* and said I should write it ten times, which is what you have to do if you spell a word wrong in our class. (Which I never had to do before.)

On the way back to my seat Otto Zimmer said, "Ha-ha, Hannah. You spelled a word wrong."

He should talk. Otto Zimmer is the *worst* speller in our class. He spells almost *every* word wrong. Otto Zimmer writes so many words ten times he's lucky he ever gets finished in time to get the bus after school.

Otto is almost *always* fresh. I felt like saying, "Shut up, Otto," but my mother always says, "If you can't say anything nice, don't say anything at all." So I didn't say anything at all.

Then the buzzer rang and the teacher had to go down to the office to see what Miss Starr wanted. Miss Starr is the new principal. She's nice.

Before she went, the teacher said Edna Mae Waller should be monitor till she got back and she also said, "No talking." But she didn't say no using the dictionary so when the door closed I went up to the dictionary and looked it up.

Was I surprised! The teacher was right and I was wrong! So I wrote *restaurateur* ten times.

But I still think it doesn't make sense.

When I told my parents after school, my father said he isn't a restaurateur *or* a restauranteur. He said he's just an ordinary guy who owns a little road stand and two gas pumps on Route 9W.

I said, "But the sign you made on the roof doesn't say Grand View Road Stand—it says Grand View Restaurant."

Then my mother said she doesn't like fancy words anyway.

My mother doesn't like *anything* fancy. Even my grandmother doesn't like anything fancy. If you bring her a fancy present she makes you take it back. She says it's not a necessity.

But I like fancy things, don't you, President Roosevelt?

Love from your friend,
Hannah

February 18, 1938

Dear Edward,

Mathilda is not the only one who likes you in the world.

I changed my mind.

I decided I like you too.

See, when I got your first letter, I thought you were being a smart aleck. I was wrong.

So I'm sorry I acted stuck up and corrected your English. If I ever get to be a real teacher I'll say good English isn't the most important thing in the world. Being kind is.

It's lucky you're good in arithmetic. Arithmetic is very important. I'm *terrible* in arithmetic—it's my worst subject. My father is terrible in arithmetic too. If he writes a check in the checkbook he always makes a mistake and my mother has to fix it. Most of the time he doesn't even remember to write it in. So my mother calls him the absent-minded professor.

My mother is good in arithmetic. She used to be a bookkeeper.

I think arithmetic is a very good thing to be good in.

Would you tell me more about your farm? I don't know anybody who lives on a farm. I always thought it would be fun. I didn't know about getting up at five o'clock in the morning to do chores.

Next time my mother yells at me to get out of that bed or she'll pull the covers off me at seven o'clock in the morning to go to school, I'll think of you out there in the dark and it will be easier for me to get up.

Your friend,
Hannah

P.S. I think any person who talks softly to a cow is a nice person. Especially if the cow is going to have a calf.

Look what I saw sticking up out of the snow today: *snowdrops!*

Edward, I am *really* sorry.

February 22, 1938

Dear Hannah,

Thanks for saying it's good I'm good in arithmetic. Because I am. It's the only thing though. I'm not good in nothing else.

Yesterday I brought home my report card and you know what I heard my father say to my mother? He said, "What are we raising here—the village idiot?" She said, "Shush" but I heard him anyway.

I got so mad I didn't talk to my father all day. He didn't even notice!

You asked would I tell you more about our farm. Don't get mad but no. I hate working on a farm so much I don't even like to talk about it.

I don't know what I'm going to be when I grow up, but I know what I *don't* want to be. I don't want to be a farmer.

Edward Winchley

P.S. Your letter was nice. The snowdrops too.

February 26, 1938

Dear Edward,

I promise never to ask you about a farm again.

About the village idiot—listen to this: My father is reading a book by a man named Albert Einstein who is supposed to be a genius. The book is so hard my father's only on page nine even though he's been reading the book all year! He just keeps reading each page over and over and says he won't turn the page till he understands it. He falls asleep with that book open every night. The last time he did that was when he read a book about the stars. My father loves the stars! He says he still doesn't know what Albert Einstein is talking about but he *wants* to know so that's why he keeps on reading.

Now what I want to tell you is this: My mother says she read an article about Albert Einstein and it said when he was a boy he was so bad in school, a teacher told his mother and father, "This boy will never amount to anything!"

So maybe you could tell your father about Albert Einstein.

Your friend,
Hannah

March 2, 1938

Dear Hannah,

That was very good about Albert Einstein.

I would like to be a genius and write a book that nobody could understand but me. Then my father would be sorry he said that. He would ask me to explain the book and I would say no.

I wonder how Albert Einstein got to be a genius. I know how he didn't get to be one. I'll bet a million dollars he wasn't a farmer.

What do you think a person has to do to become a genius?

Well, I have to stop now. It's time to go out and feed the chickens.

Edward Winchley

P.S. Boy, are chickens stupid! One chicken pecks another chicken and when the rest of them see a red spot (blood) they all start chasing the chicken who got pecked. They run so fast, sometimes they get a heart attack. I'm not fooling either—chickens can get a heart attack and lots of other things too. I'm glad I'm a person and not a chicken.

March 6, 1938

Dear Edward,

I don't know what a person has to do to become a genius, but I can tell you one thing. You have to read a lot of books.

Not everybody who reads a lot of books becomes a genius. Most people become just regular people like you and me. But other people, like Albert Einstein, start out with reading books, I'm sure.

Then the books give them things to think about and when some people think, they get ideas to write a book of their own with new ideas that weren't even in the books they read. Then people like my father get to read the books and fall asleep trying to figure them out. This is just books by geniuses, like Albert Einstein.

Other books, most of them, you read for pleasure. That's what my teacher, Miss Hopkins, says and I think she's right. My favorite thing in the world to do is read a book. I read *Heidi,* which I love, then I read another book, then I read *Heidi* again. If I stopped reading *Heidi* in between the other books, I'd be able to read twice as many books, but the thing is I *like* reading *Heidi.* So I do. When I read it, I forget where I am (mostly I'm in my secret place at the top of the mountain that nobody knows about but me). I feel like I'm in Switzerland with Heidi and her grandfather and a boy named Peter and a girl named Clara and a horrible lady named Fräulein Rottenmeier. I *hate* Fräulein Rottenmeier.

You really ought to *try* reading a book sometime, Edward. You don't know what you're missing!

Your friend,
Hannah

P.S. I'm glad you're not a chicken too.

March 7, 1938

Dear Edward,

And another thing.

Right after I mailed your letter yesterday I thought of something you might like to know because you said you'd like to be a genius and write a book nobody could understand but you.

We had a real author come to our school for assembly last week.

He told us all about writing a book.

Now, listen to this: He said when he was our age he used to get mad when his teachers corrected his mistakes on his papers. He said he used to go home and throw the papers out and never read what the teachers told him was wrong.

When he decided to become a writer, he was sorry he did that. Because he said when you write a book you send it to the publisher. The publisher is the place that makes the book into a book. And up at the publisher's, there are people called editors. They read your book and decide whether it's good enough. If it's not good enough they just send it back to you and don't correct you.

But if they think it's good enough, they *do* correct you and if you make mistakes in English you have to fix them! That author said he wishes now he had listened to his teachers instead of throwing the papers away. He said he could have learned something! And he said we should listen to our teachers and not get mad when they make corrections on our papers.

The reason I'm telling you this is I thought you should

know: Even if you write a book that nobody can understand but you, you still can't write double negatives. They will correct you, Edward!

So if you want any tips on this subject, I'd be glad to help you.

Your friend,
Hannah

P.S. It would be easy because on a little rolled-up piece of paper in a cubby in my desk, right next to the cubby where I keep President Roosevelt's stamps in a walnut shell, don't get mad but I have a list of all your double negatives. Because remember when you said "I don't even want to know"? I thought maybe someday you *would* want to know. Then I would have the list ready.

March 13, 1938

Dear Miss Missy,

I would *love* to know how to be a crackerjack secretary!

I eat a box of Cracker Jacks every week. I don't really like them but I get them for the prizes. I open the box and hold my breath and wish for a ring.

Other things I might be besides a secretary when I grow up are a teacher or an artist.

Now I want to tell you something that happened here the day after I got your letter. Because I have a question to ask you at the end. And I'll draw a picture too so you can tell me if you think it's good enough to be an artist when I grow up in case I'm not a secretary or a teacher.

The day after your letter came, a famous person stopped at the Grand View Restaurant! If my mother didn't have the rule "No customers in our private bathroom," we could have been in the papers—on page one! Instead Billy Allen's Tavern was. Billy Allen's is the next place down the road. It's a bar!

Here's what happened:

I was outside seeing if I could keep my balance on the edge of the long brick flower box my father built in front of the ladies' and men's rooms next to the garage.

All of a sudden I saw a fancy car drive up in front of the restaurant. It was the longest car I ever saw. My father said it's called a limousine.

A man in a gray uniform got out of the front seat. He was a chauffeur—just like in the movies! He went into the restaurant.

I was in such a hurry to see the limousine up close I

almost lost my balance and fell into the flower box. But I didn't. I ran over near the limousine and was going to go up close and peek in to see the inside.

But then I saw a person's nose in the backseat. That's all that was showing in the window: a nose, sideways. So I didn't go any closer.

I ran into the restaurant. The chauffeur was talking to my mother.

"Madame would like to use your ladies' room," he said.

My mother pointed to the long brick flower box and to the signs my father made. The signs say LADIES and GENTLEMEN.

"The ladies' room is out there," she said.

The chauffeur went back out to the car and the back window rolled down a little ways. He talked to the nose. I heard a loud clap. It sounded just like the ladies in the lunchroom at school. They clap hands if we talk too loud.

My father came out of the kitchen and said to my mother, "Look at that limousine! That must be somebody famous!"

My mother said, "The ladies' room is still outside."

The chauffeur came back in. "Madame does not use public rest rooms," he said. "Madame would like to use *your* rest room."

"Our rest room is private," said my mother.

The chauffeur went back out. *Clap, clap!* I heard it again.

"Maybe . . ." said my father.

The chauffeur came back in.

"Madame said to tell you," said the chauffeur, "that if you knew who Madame is . . ."

"It doesn't make any difference," said my mother. "I don't play favorites. The ladies' room is still outside."

The chauffeur went back out. He talked to the nose again. *Clap, clap!* Louder than all the ladies in the lunchroom put together.

Then the back window rolled up, the chauffeur got into the front seat and slammed the door, and the big long car drove off so fast the gravel scrunched up under the tires and dust went up into the air.

I ran back out. All I saw was the back of the big long car driving away.

I ran back inside.

My mother and father were having an argument.

"I'm sure that was a famous person," said my father.

"Famous, shmamous," said my mother. "Everybody is the same. Our bathroom is private."

"Sometimes we could make an exception," said my father.

"Whoever she is, she's snooty," said my mother. "What's wrong with public rest rooms? She's a cheapskate too—she didn't even buy a pack of gum for a nickel."

I ran out and balanced myself on the edge of the long brick flower box again.

I don't like it when my mother and father have an argument. I always think I have to decide who's right, but I never can. They both seem a little bit right to me.

Then, when the *Nyack Journal News* came out, there was a great big picture of a lady on page one. Her whole face, not just her nose.

A headline all the way across the top said MADAME CHIANG KAI-SHEK STOPS AT BILLY ALLEN'S TAVERN.

"Look at this!" said my father. "I told you it was someone famous—Madame Chiang Kai-shek!"

"I know who she is," I said. "My teacher told us. Her husband is a general in China. Generalissimo Chiang Kai-shek."

"We could have been in the papers!" said my father. "Page one!"

My mother said she didn't care to be in the papers. "Page anything.

"Our bathroom is private," she said. "We have little enough privacy as it is, living in back of a restaurant. People can see us right through the fish tank!"

Billy Allen called my father up. He invited us to see a big framed picture of Madame Chiang Kai-shek he hung up over the bar.

We didn't go.

I wanted to see the picture but my mother said we don't go to bars. She said it would be all smoky and noisy.

My father looked gloomy. He kept studying the papers.

"Ah, who cares?" he finally said. "Chiang Kai-shek is a gangster."

And he started to laugh.

"What's the joke?" said my mother.

"Everybody will think Madame Chiang stopped off for a beer!" he said.

My mother looked at him—and then she started laughing too.

When they laugh I like it much better than when they argue.

I ran and got my dog Skippy and raced him up the mountain.

"Skippy!" I yelled. "We were *almost* in the papers!"

When we got to the top, I thought, *I saw a famous person's nose—in person!*

So that's what happened the day after your letter came, Miss Missy. And my question is: Did Madame Chiang Kai-shek ever come to the White House in her limousine with her chauffeur? If she did, did Mrs. Roosevelt let her use *their* private bathroom? And did she clap?

Your friend,
Hannah

P.S. Here's my drawing:

March 14, 1938

Dear Aggie,

I joined Bunny Hunnicutt's club. It's called the GWMDTOGTAMN Club.

Only certain people can be invited to join. You have to have special qualifications. I have those qualifications so I got invited.

I'm sorry to tell you that you would not be able to join this club.

Love,
Hannah

P.S. I was in the woods today—that place on the River Road across from my secret cove, where you and I used to look for violets on Mother's Day—and I found a lot of pussy willows. They felt just like velvet!

This is my fourteenth letter.

THE WHITE HOUSE
1600 Pennsylvania Avenue
Washington, D.C.

March 15, 1938

Dear Hannah,

Thank you for your letter of February 15.

If I were you, I would not worry too much about missing one spelling word. You are still the best speller in your class and that is excellent. To be excellent is good enough--one need not be perfect. It has been my experience that perfect people are sometimes boring!

Enclosed find a stamp from Switzerland. I thought you might find the sight of a bear walking upright, just like a person, amusing.

So don't give the word you missed another thought. Just do your best at all times, my dear--your best is good enough--and everything will come out all right.

Sincerely, your friend,

Franklin Delano Roosevelt

Franklin Delano Roosevelt

FDR:MAL

March 20, 1938

Dear Grandma,

Don't be disappointed in me, but I missed a spelling word: *restaurateur.* I had to write it ten times. I felt terrible, but President Roosevelt said not to. I asked him if he could spell it, but he forgot to say. He sent me a bear.

My aunt Becky is knitting me something again. She called on the telephone to remind me that she's knitting me some guess-whats. I don't like it when Aunt Becky knits me those itchy bumpy things. When she finishes she always writes me a letter and says, "What should I knit next?"

I never know what to say. Once I asked Ma if I could write a letter and say, *Dear Aunt Becky, Please knit nothing next.* She said no.

Did my aunt Becky ever knit you something? If she did, was it itchy and bumpy? And when she finished, did she say, "What should I knit next?"

Hello to Grandpa.

Love,
Hannah

March 24, 1938

Dear Hannah,

Yes, your aunt Becky did once knit something for Grandpa and me. She came to see the candy store. With her she had a measuring tape. The whole time she was here she was measuring. After she went home, we received a telephone call. She said, "I am knitting you something—guess what?" A week later we received a package. She knitted a cover for the malted milk machine and another for the big jar of maraschino cherries! "Jackets," she called them. She said put them on at night before we close the store to keep the dust off.

What kind of dust comes at night?

But we didn't have to worry about itchy and bumpy because we didn't have to wear them. She didn't say, "What should I knit next?" because after all she is not on our side of the family so she probably figures two guess-whats were enough.

I think you are your aunt Becky's dear, as well as ours, and that's why she knits you things. Her heart is in the right place and she means well.

Listen, Hannah, we are never disappointed in you. We like you just the way you are.

What kind of word is *restaurateur* anyway? It's too fancy for me.

Love from Grandpa also,
Grandma

P.S. What kind of a bear did President Roosevelt send you? A teddy bear?

March 27, 1938

Dear Grandma,

The bear President Roosevelt sent me was on a stamp. I forgot to tell you. It was from Switzerland.

Aunt Becky called again last night. She said she is 20% finished with the guess-whats. My mother always tells me Aunt Becky's heart is in the right place too. But my mother doesn't have to wear the things she knits—*I* do. Aunt Becky said, "When you see these guess-whats, you'll faint."

She always says that. Once my father almost fainted when she sent him a knitted jacket for his cigar box! He said to my mother, "How am I supposed to get the box open with this thing on it?" My mother said, "Maybe that's the idea. Maybe you should keep it closed."

My mother doesn't like my father's cigars. They're called White Owls. She calls them stinkers. She thinks smoking isn't good for you.

She never said anything about Grandpa's pipe though. I like Grandpa's pipe. It smells nice.

White Owl cigars don't smell so nice but I like them anyway because they have paper rings and my father always saves me the rings. Also he blows smoke rings up to the ceiling for me and I like to watch them float.

Well, that's all for now, Grandma.

Love,
Hannah

P.S. A restaurateur is a person who owns a restaurant. My father is one but he says he's not. He thinks it's too fancy too.

April 2, 1938

Dear President Roosevelt,

Thank you for the stamp from Switzerland.

The walking bear is really funny. He looks like he is swinging his arms. I put him in the walnut shell in my cubby with the kangaroo from Australia, the giraffe from Tanganyika, and the elephant from Liberia. So now they can keep each other company.

President Roosevelt, do you have an autograph book? I do.

Wait till I tell you what a man who signed my autograph book made up about you.

The kids in school mostly write the same things in autograph books. Like:

Remember Grant, remember Lee.
The heck with them, remember me.

or

I love you, I love you, I love you so well,
If I had a peanut I'd give you the shell.

One girl in my class wrote this:

To Hannah, the other member of the GWMDTOGTAMN Club,
Bunny Hunnicutt

Because once last year when our teacher Miss Pepper asked us our middle name, Bunny and I were the only ones who didn't have any. When we found that out, we both decided to ask our mothers why we didn't get a middle name.

Our mothers both said the same thing: "I didn't think of it."

So then Bunny said we should have a club: Girls Whose Mothers Didn't Think Of Giving Them A Middle Name. That's what GWMDTOGTAMN stands for.

The only thing is there's not much to do in a club like that. So I told Bunny we should make lists of middle names and pick one out. She picked Veronica. I picked Ginger. (For Ginger Rogers.)

Aggie Branagan who doesn't answer my letters and be my pen pal has *two* middle names! She wrote in my autograph book before they moved:

To Hannah from Agnes Maria Theresa Branagan
You are my best friend forever.

Love, Aggie

I guess she forgot about that.

Sometimes I get autographs from customers at the Grand View Restaurant. I only ask special customers though.

Like today I asked a man because he was funny.

He came in when I was playing rolls on our piano after school. On our piano, you can play a roll with the keys flat or you can push a button and make the keys go up and down. When I do that I put my hands on the keys and make believe I'm playing.

The man came in with a lady when I was playing "On the Good Ship Lollipop," my favorite roll. I heard him say, "That girl can really play!" So then I had to tell the truth, that it was a player piano.

I waited on them. He had a hamburger—rare, the way you like them. She had a hot dog.

He told us he writes rhymes for a living. He said he could make them up "one-two-three!"

So I got my autograph book and said, "Make a rhyme about me!" He asked me my name. Then he wrote:

If your name is Hannah
You will play the piano.

He signed his name *Harry O. Burns.*

I said, "Mr. Burns, I hope you won't be insulted but *Hannah* doesn't rhyme with *piano. Hannah* rhymes with *piana. Piano* rhymes with *Hanno.*"

He looked surprised. Then he laughed. He said, "Okay, I'll write another. Tell me some things you like to do."

I said, "Read, draw, write letters, and tap-dance."

So then he wrote:

If your name is not Frances,
You will do fancy dances.

Isn't that good, President Roosevelt? He made it up one-two-three!

He said he wrote what my name was *not* (Frances) because the only word that really rhymes with *Hannah* is *banana.*

Then I asked him to write a rhyme about you. He said he likes you too, just the way we do. Everybody likes you, President Roosevelt! And one-two-three he wrote:

Hitch your star
To FDR!

Isn't that wonderful? I asked him to write that in my autograph book too.

And when he left, he gave me a quarter for a tip.

My father said he must have been rich.

My mother said he was showing off.

Love from your friend,
Hannah

P.S. Speaking of stars, remember when you told us that Mrs. Roosevelt's uncle President Theodore Roosevelt said that about the square deal? Well, my mother read an article called "Teddy Roosevelt" and the article told two other famous things he said. One was "Speak softly and carry a big stick." The other was "Keep your feet on the ground and your eyes on the stars."

My mother liked the second one so much she copied it down. Then she showed it to my father and said to him, "No wonder you love the stars so much. You have your eyes on the stars"—she said that's why she married him—"but the trouble is you have your *feet* on the stars too." He said he doesn't. She said he does. She said she has to be the anchor so he won't sail away up into the sky like a kite.

For the first time, my father and I didn't think the same thing is funny.

April 3, 1938

Dear Agnes Maria Theresa Branagan,

Did you forget what you wrote in my autograph book just before you moved?

You wrote, *You are my best friend forever.*

Your best friend forever is still waiting for a letter from you, Aggie.

Love,
Hannah

P.S. This is my fifteenth letter. And just in case you were wanting to know, the reason you can't join the GWMDTOGTAMN Club is you have two middle names.

And *furthermore,* Aggie. I am starting to get mad. I am starting to get *so* mad. Who cried when you came up to the Grand View Restaurant? Did *I* cry? I did not cry. *You* cried. Who said, "You won't write to me. You'll forget me"? Did *I* say that? No, *you* said that.

I don't even know why I still want you for a friend, Aggie. Well, just the same I do. And I'm already sorry I said what I just said. But I don't take it back. Because it's all true.

April 1, 1938

Dear Hannah,

Well, I read a book. The teacher said I would get zero in reading if I didn't.

So I read that book you said in your first letter had a girl in it who lives in Kansas. *The Wizard of Oz.* I even read some of it to my sister. She liked it.

Then just when I was glad I wouldn't get zero in reading, the teacher said I had to write a book report to prove I read the whole book.

I never wrote a book report before. Here is what I wrote:

> The book I read was *The Wizard of Oz.*
> It wasn't bad.

The teacher said she didn't call that a book report. She said two lines was not enough. Just like when you said you didn't call my first letter a letter. Two lines was not enough then. Two lines is not enough now.

I don't know what everybody wants from me.

Now I have to write it over or I'll get zero in writing a book report.

I was wondering if you could help me write a book report.

Maybe I could help you in arithmetic sometime.

Edward (Two Lines) Winchley

April 4, 1938

Dear Edward Two Lines,

That was a very good joke.

Now, about the book report.

I can't write it for you because your teacher would know. Just like you couldn't do my arithmetic because then *my* teacher would know. Teachers are like mothers—*they always know!*

But I can help give you some tips. I'm expecting a letter from President Roosevelt's secretary and she's going to give me some tips on how to be a good secretary in case I want to be a secretary when I grow up. So I'll give you some tips on how to write a good book report right now.

Tell the name of the book. Tell the name of the author. *The Wizard of Oz* was written by L. Frank Baum.

Tell if you think he's a good writer. Tell the names of all the characters in the book. Tell what they did. Tell where they went. Tell who they were looking for. Tell what they finally found. Tell how they treated each other. Tell about their feelings.

Tell that you read some to your sister. Tell that she liked it.

Read some to a friend. Then you can even tell that your friend liked it.

By that time, Edward, you'll have so many lines your teacher will leave you alone.

And don't forget to tell me how it turns out.

Your friend,
Hannah

April 4, 1938

Dear Hannah,

I liked your drawing and think you could be an artist when you grow up. Perhaps a cartoonist!

But if you should choose to be a secretary, here are the tips I promised:

Before you look for a job, go to secretarial school and learn to use a typewriter. Practice and practice until you can type very fast, because often when a secretary applies for a job, she is asked, ''How many words a minute can you type?'' Learn shorthand so you can take dictation. Practice doing that until you can do it very well too.

When you decide that you have become the very best you can be, look in the newspapers in the section called ''Classified Ads.'' Look under Secretary.

When you have found a job, here is the most important tip of all: Listen very carefully when your boss dictates a letter. Even more important than the way you type or take shorthand is to listen to how he talks, what he says, and the way he says it. Study the letters and study your boss. After a while you'll realize you could write a letter for him, if he wants you to, even if he isn't there, because you'll know what he would say and how he would say it.

Suppose he doesn't feel well, for example, and he wants to go home and go to bed. You can show him some letters that came in the mail and that have to be answered, and he can tell you which ones he wants you to answer and which ones not. And then he can go home and go to bed, and you can write the letters for him.

I hope these tips will be of help to you someday.

As to your questions about Madame C.: Although she has not been here to date, I am certain that sooner or later she will. I shall recognize her immediately by her nose, thanks to your drawing. And I shall be sure to have available several sets of earplugs.

I give your mother credit for sticking to her guns about privacy.

Here in the White House, on the third floor, I have my own private quarters in a very cozy room with slanted ceilings. I too value my privacy and wouldn't like to have it invaded.

If you have any more questions or stories to tell, I'm always glad to lend an ear.

Sincerely yours,

Missy LeHand

Missy LeHand

April 8, 1938

Dear Hannah,

The Wizard of Oz

This book was written by a man named L. Frank Baum. I think L. Frank Baum is a very good writer.

The characters in the book were Dorothy and her dog Toto and the Tin Woodman and the Cowardly Lion and the Scarecrow. Dorothy met them when she blew away in Kansas in a cyclone. They had plenty of problems. There was a nasty witch and a nice one. They followed the Yellow Brick Road. They were looking for the Wizard of Oz. He was supposed to know everything. He wasn't supposed to be afraid of nothing. The Cowardly Lion was afraid of everything. The Tin Woodman was worried he would get rusty if he didn't get oiled. The Scarecrow was scared of catching on fire. Dorothy wished she could get home to her aunt Em and her uncle Henry. When they finally found the wizard, he was more scared than they were even though in the beginning he made believe he wasn't. Dorothy and the Scarecrow and the Cowardly Lion and the Tin Woodman were all very nice to each other. So in the end Dorothy told the wizard it was okay to be afraid because everybody is. And then they all felt better.

I read some to my sister. She liked it.

I read some to my friend Mathilda. She loved it.

So that is all about *The Wizard of Oz*.

by Edward Winchley

Thanks for the tips on how to write a book report, Hannah. The teacher said I had one mistake. It was that same double negative stuff. She said I should say, "He wasn't afraid of *anything*" instead of "He wasn't afraid of nothing"—like you! So now in case I ever try to write a book like Albert Einstein, I guess you better give me those tips on double negatives. I didn't know about those editors. They sound like *teachers!* And I didn't get mad because you rolled up my mistakes in a cubbyhole. But what did you mean about stamps and President Roosevelt and a walnut shell?

The teacher wrote *Good!* on top of my paper. She wrote it *big*. In *red!* It was the first red *Good!* of my life. Then she made me stand up and read my report in front of the class.

My knees were knocking together. My teeth were knocking together. I hope nobody heard.

When I said, "I read some to my friend Mathilda," one of the boys, Charlie Rehnquist, yelled, "Ooh, ooh—Edward has a girlfriend!" The teacher told him to be quiet but on the way home from school, on the bus he said it again.

I closed my eyes and made believe I was sleeping. I fall asleep in class a lot because I get up so early in the morning to do chores and I fall asleep on the bus too sometimes, so when I made believe I was sleeping Charlie Rehnquist thought I really *was* sleeping and he shut up. That's good because sometimes when he does that the other guys on the bus start yelling too and they won't stop. Is that what you meant when you said the boys on your bus act like a bunch of wild animals?

This is the longest letter I ever wrote in my life.

Edward Winchley

P.S. My mother showed my father the paper with the red *Good!* on the top. And you know what he said? He said, "Well, Edward, the worm is turning!" How would you like it if your father called you a worm?

April 6, 1938

Dear Hannah,

Hello from Aunt Becky again!

I am now 40% finished with the guess-whats.

I'll give you a little hint. I am enclosing a piece of wool to show you the color. Pink. Every girl likes pink.

When I'm 60% finished, I'll give another hint besides the color. At 80%, more hints.

When I'm 100% finished, if I have any wool left over, I'll make a jacket for my little sweetie pie thoroughbred Poopala-darling. Pink would look nice on a teeny gray poodle, don't you think?

Well, it's time for me to turn on the *Metropolitan Opera of the Air.* Today I'll sing along with *La Forza del Destino.* And while I sing, I'll keep knitting. So don't worry—I won't forget your guess-whats. I'll be finished before you know it.

Love and kisses,
Aunt Becky

April 8, 1938

Dear Aunt Becky,

I know you won't forget my guess-whats. And *that's* why I worry.

And this girl does not like pink. Pink is for babies. I like *red.*

I don't think any color would look nice on Poopala-darling. She looks like a little gray rat with curls.

Please don't bring her here again. The last time, poor Skippy had to sleep down in the basement so that bratty poodle wouldn't get an infection from a mutt. It wasn't fair. Skippy hasn't got any infections. He may be a mutt but he's a *healthy* mutt.

I don't see what's so wonderful about a thoroughbred anyway. All she does is yap and I'm not allowed to make any sudden movements because of her heart condition. It's very hard not to make any sudden movements.

I never heard of a dog with a heart condition anyhow. I heard of *chickens* that get heart attacks but never a dog.

So next time you visit, Aunt Becky, come alone. Don't bring poodles and don't bring knitting.

Love,
Hannah

P.S. If I ever mailed this letter my mother would kill me.

April 10, 1938

Dear Edward,

I wouldn't like it if my father called me a worm. But I don't think your father meant you were a worm. I think "The worm turns" is just an expression. Sometimes it's even a compliment. Maybe he just meant he liked your book report.

It was good. You should be proud of yourself. And just one double negative isn't so bad. I'm glad you're not mad because I put your mistakes in a cubbyhole.

What I meant about President Roosevelt and the stamps is I wrote him some letters. He wrote me some answers! And he sent me some stamps from his stamp collection. So I put them in a walnut shell, and they're in the cubbyhole in my desk right next to your mistakes. I'll send you some tips in my next letter. You'd probably like a little rest after all that reading and writing.

Yes, that Charlie Rehnquist on your bus sounds just like the wild animals on *our* bus! I wish they'd all run away from school and start a zoo someplace far away. Then we could have some peace and quiet.

I hate the school bus.

It's so *noisy*. I don't mind the noise from talking—I mind the noise from bullying and teasing.

It's the boys. Not all of them but most of them. They bully and tease each other all the time. The minute they get on the bus, they start.

They pick one person. If he doesn't show that it scares him, they stop. But if he shows that it scares him, they get worse.

Right now there's a new boy, Joseph Spratt. He's not a bully or a tease like a lot of the other boys on the bus. He's quiet.

One day one of the boys, Marty Clark—he's the ringleader—yelled, "Spratt, Spratt, the scaredy-cat, fifty bullets in his hat!"

Secretly *I'm* a scaredy-cat, Edward. So I don't like to hear that.

Joseph Spratt didn't say anything. He just smiled.

Then some other boys said it too.

"Spratt, Spratt, the scaredy-cat, fifty bullets in his hat!"

Joseph Spratt still didn't say anything—he just kept smiling. But his lips looked a little bit wobbly.

Then all the boys on the bus yelled together, "Spratt, Spratt, the scaredy-cat, fifty bullets in his hat!"

They were yelling *so loud!*

And finally Joseph Spratt started to cry.

He shouldn't have cried in front of them. I knew just what was going to happen.

They yelled it louder and louder. He cried more. The more he cried, the more they yelled.

I wanted to tell him, "Joseph, don't cry till you get off the bus," but I don't even know Joseph Spratt. And even if I did, he wouldn't have heard me. Those boys are really loud yellers.

I always thought, *Whew! I'm glad I'm not a boy. All they ever do is tease each other and see if they can make each other cry.* And I also used to think, *I'm glad I'm a girl.* They don't usually try to make the girls cry.

But now there's even a girl they make cry. Her name is Lottie Biddle.

Lottie Biddle cries at almost everything. Sometimes she cries if somebody just looks at her.

One day in the middle of yelling, "Spratt, Spratt, the scaredy-cat . . ." one of the boys noticed that Lottie Biddle was crying. I don't know if she was crying because she felt sorry for Joseph Spratt, like I do (except I don't cry) or if she was crying about something else. I tried to send her a message with my eyes: "Lottie, don't let them see you cry . . ."

But it was too late.

Marty Clark stopped yelling, "Spratt, Spratt, the scaredy-cat . . ." and he yelled, "Bawl Baby Biddle!"

The other boys stopped yelling, "Spratt, Spratt, the scaredy-cat . . ." and switched to "Bawl Baby Biddle" too.

It was worse than Joseph Spratt. When Joseph cries, he doesn't make a sound. Tears just drop out of his eyes and roll down his cheeks.

But Lottie cries out loud. The louder they yell, "Bawl Baby Biddle!" the louder she cries.

Today I decided I can't stand those boys on the bus another minute.

They were yelling so loud that when the driver stopped at the light at the corner of Broadway and Cornelison Avenue, he turned his head and said, "Will youse kids shut up?" That's when I got off the bus.

The driver doesn't let you get off at a stop that's not your stop without a note from your mother giving permission. I didn't have a note from my mother giving permission.

I gave myself permission. And I walked the rest of the way home.

The bus got to the Grand View Restaurant before I did, so my mother thought I missed it.

When I got to the door she said, "What happened?" I told her.

And I told her, "I'm not going to school on the bus anymore. I'm walking."

At first my mother and father didn't want me to because Route 9W doesn't have a sidewalk. But Cornelison Avenue and Broadway do.

I told them they let me walk to the library and that's almost as far as school. And I'm very careful on Route 9W.

So they gave me a note with permission to walk because if you're a bus rider and you walk to school you have to have a note with permission for that too. I had to take the note to Miss Starr, the principal. She said, "How long would you like to keep walking, Hannah?" I said, "Forever."

Does your bus driver tell the boys to shut up? (I hate "shut up," but they deserve it.) Does he say "youse kids"? Our driver says "youse kids" all the time. It's bad English. At least you never said that, Edward. Not to me, anyway.

Your friend,
Hannah

P.S. I feel sorry for Lottie Biddle and Joseph Spratt, but I'd rather *die* than cry in front of a bully—wouldn't you?

April 10, 1938

Dear Miss Missy,

Thanks for all those tips you sent me on how to be a good secretary. I folded them up and put them in a cubbyhole on my desk on one side of President Roosevelt's stamps in a walnut shell. On the other side of President Roosevelt is a cubbyhole filled with mistakes made by a boy I know in Kansas. I promised to give *him* tips—I got the idea of tips from you—on how to talk English without double negatives.

And thanks for the idea about me being a cartoonist if I'm not a secretary or a teacher when I grow up. I'd really like that—especially since I'm the only girl in my class whose father gets a newspaper without comics.

I keep asking my father to get a newspaper that has the comics but he says he likes *The New York Times.* Also the *Herald Tribune* and a Jewish newspaper I don't even know the name of. But they don't have comics either.

Soon I'll try to draw a cartoon. When I do, I'll send it to you because you gave me the idea.

Your friend,
Hannah

April 11, 1938

Dear Grandma,

I'm writing you a special letter just to say thank you for something I never thought of thanking you for before.

It's for when you say, "We like you just the way you are." The other day I was thinking: You always say that to me but I never told you how much I like it.

The reason I like it is that grown-ups hardly ever say that to children. Mostly grown-ups tell us they would like us to make improvements. Just the way we are is usually not good enough.

So I want you to know I appreciate that, Grandma.

Love to you and Grandpa,
Hannah

April 12, 1938

Dear Miss Missy,

Here is my comic strip that I made up. It has a name: *Copycat.*

I really like dogs better than cats but I never heard of a copydog. So I made it a copycat. If you like it, I'll make you another one.

Love from your friend,
Hannah

P.S. Today I saw a crocus.

April 12, 1938

Dear Hannah,

Your bus sounds even worse than ours!

About that boy Joseph Spratt. Tell him Edward Winchley has a tip for him (like you had tips for me when I did the book report). (And like you're going to give me more of so I'll have good English in case I ever write a book.) Tell him to make believe he's sleeping. If it works with Charlie Rehnquist it could work with the bullies on your bus too. Maybe.

I don't blame you for walking home. I'd like to do that too, but if I did I'd have to walk five miles and then I'd be late for my afternoon chores.

I don't cry in front of bullies either. I don't even cry in front of myself—I'm a *boy!* But even if I wanted to cry, I wouldn't have time to cry. I'm too busy doing chores.

We are having a big frost. My grandpa is very worried about his fruit trees.

What's new on Route 9W?

Edward Winchley, the Worm Who Turned

P.S. I wish I had a stamp collection. And I never say "youse" to nobody.

April 15, 1938

Dear Edward,

You are really getting funny!

I wish I could send you my stamps. To tell you the truth, if the stamps weren't from President Roosevelt, I *would* send them to you because I never really was interested in collecting stamps. (Maybe it's because there is a boy in my class who collects stamps and I can't stand him. His name is Otto Zimmer and he gives me a pain.) But I have an idea: I'll trace the stamps I got so far so you can see them. I got four:

Hope you like them.

Now, about what you said about boys can't cry: I don't agree with that. I know you didn't make it up because I hear people say it here too. Who started that is what I'd like to know. When I grow up, if I have a son I'll tell him he *can.* I'll say laugh when something is funny and cry when something is sad.

Now, Edward, I'm going to tell you a story because you asked, "What's new on Route 9W?" Don't worry, this isn't a story like in a book, but something that really happened this week.

A man came walking up Route 9W. He had a knapsack on his back.

He stopped where our fence begins and looked at the ground.

Then he went to Skippy's doghouse and petted Skippy.

And then he came over to the counter and asked if we had any work he could do for something to eat.

Once I heard my father and Mr. Branagan, Aggie's father, having an argument over the men who come to your door and ask for something to eat.

Mr. Branagan said those men are just bums who don't want to work.

My father said because of hard times those men can't find a job and you shouldn't call them bums because it could happen to anybody.

Later my mother said that if Mr. Branagan worked for another paperhanger and wasn't in business for himself, *he'd* be out of a job because he leaves all those lumps of paste under the wallpaper. She said would he then call himself a bum?

Anyhow, the men who ask for something to eat are called hoboes by some people because they travel around and jump on trains and ride to other places to see if they can find jobs there. And they're called bums by other people.

I don't think it's nice for people to call other people bums.

My mother and father always give them a cheese sandwich, a cup of coffee, and a piece of apple pie.

When the man came walking up Route 9W with the

knapsack on his back the other day, I was sitting at the counter drawing with my new box of Crayolas that my grandmother gave me from the candy store. It's the biggest box of crayons I ever saw and has every color in the world, including gold and silver. I love new crayons because they still have points, don't you? I was also reading *Heidi*. I like to draw a little, read a little.

My mother was putting salt and pepper in the salt and pepper shakers.

My father said he was going to take his fish out of the bathtub, where he keeps them when he cleans his fish tank, which my mother hates, and he said the man could help him do that.

I started to say, "Hey, *I* like to do that," but I only got as far as "Hey" because my mother said, "Hay is for horses" and my father looked at me like he was trying to tell me something. I figured out what it was. He wanted to give the man some work so he wouldn't be embarrassed about asking for something to eat. So I read some more *Heidi* and then I drew more goldfish.

I drew the ones we have the most of: the orange ones with the gold underneath. I also drew the black ones and the white ones with the pop-eyes.

When all the fish were back in the fish tank, I went into the kitchen and made the man a cheese sandwich with a pickle on the side, and my mother made him a cup of coffee. And I got a piece of Mrs. Wagner's apple pie out of the glass case and put it on the counter next to the sandwich and coffee.

Then I finished my picture and the man ate the sandwich.

"That's a fine picture of the fish," he said. "You're a good artist."

So I went over to the ice cream box and got a vanilla Mel-o-rol and unwrapped it and put it on top of his pie.

"Pie à la mode!" he said. "Wow! It's a long time since I've had that!"

He saw my *Heidi* and said it was his little sister's favorite book. I told him how I read it in between every other library book.

When he finished, he took his dishes into the kitchen and washed them himself!

Then he came back out and opened his knapsack and right next to my Crayolas he put a sketch pad and some colored pencils. He sat down and looked at me.

And then he drew my picture—and it looked just like me! *He* was an artist—a *real* one! My mother and father couldn't get over it. He asked me my name and then he drew another picture of me. He wrote *Hannah* on both drawings and on one of them he signed his name: Franklin Elliot. He had the same first name as President Roosevelt! Isn't that a coincidence?

He gave one picture to me and the other he put inside his sketch pad. I saw more drawings in there and asked if I could see.

There were girls and boys and grown-ups—and even cats and dogs! He said he used to make a living as a portrait artist but on account of hard times nobody has money to spend on portraits anymore so he just travels all around and takes any kind of jobs he can get, which is hardly any.

Then he said he had to hop a train to look for work,

but first he wanted to show us something where our fence begins.

We all went out and he petted Skippy again and then he showed us something on the ground that just looked like a bunch of squiggly lines to me. He said hoboes scratch messages to each other on the ground—in code. The message said, *Stop here, good eats.* He said we were so nice to him he'd rub it out. Just then we heard a bang—thunder!—and it started to rain.

We ran to go back in and the man said thanks, he'd better be on his way.

My mother said it was raining too hard to be outside and he said he was used to being out in all kinds of weather. But then there was a crash of lightning and my father said it was dangerous to walk on Route 9W because of the tall trees and he should come in and wait out the storm. We took Skippy in too. Skippy's afraid of thunder and lightning. It makes him shiver.

Skippy really liked that man though. The man said we should call him Franklin. He said he used to have a dog. Then he made two little drawings of Skippy, one for us and one he put in his sketch pad with the others.

I saw that inside his knapsack were a lot of tubes of paint and brushes. He saw me peeking.

He said, "A turtle's shell is his home. I lost my home but I kept my paints—so now *I'm* like a turtle, but instead of a shell on my back, I've got my knapsack." He said he tries to make at least one drawing a day even if it's just the other guys riding the boxcars on the train with him.

He kept saying he should go but it kept raining harder. My mother and father said it was okay to sit it out but he said he felt embarrassed unless there was something he could do to feel useful.

My father got an idea. He showed Franklin the book-shelves he built across the top and down the sides of the opening between the living room and the bedrooms.

"I got carried away when I built them," my father said. "There are more shelves than we have books. So I made these little cabinet doors to cover the shelves that are empty and I thought I'd paint the doors to look like books. But then I didn't know *how* to paint books."

"I can paint books there," said Franklin. He took out his paints and brushes and while it was pouring outside, my mother and father and Skippy and I watched and Franklin painted on the cabinet doors. When he finished, the doors didn't look like doors anymore—they looked like rows of books. He made them all different colors, nice and bright. They looked better than real books!

He said it would take a couple of days to dry so not to touch it or it might smear. So my father took Skippy out to his office in the garage—my father's office, not Skippy's—so we wouldn't have to worry about the paint getting smeared from Skippy's paws or his tail or his nose.

You should see my father's office, Edward. In it he has a great big rolltop desk just like the one in my bedroom. (Both those desks and the player piano were here when we bought the restaurant.) He likes to sit at his desk and write long long letters, mostly to the editor of *The New York Times*. He writes letters whenever he reads something in the paper he doesn't agree with. He must not agree with a lot of things because he's always writing letters.

The letters are so long he has to put two stamps on the envelope. One letter was seventeen pages!

Every day my father looks first to see if his latest letter is in the papers. It never is. He always says to my mother, "They just print letters from professors. Why don't they print letters from an ordinary guy—like me?"

My mother says, "Maybe they just print letters that are an ordinary length—like one page. Did you ever think of writing one page instead of seventeen?"

My father says, "I have a lot to say."

So anyway, when my father got back from taking Skippy out to the garage, Franklin was putting his knapsack on to go, but my father said, "You can't go now—it's raining harder than before."

And my mother said he should stay and have supper—we never had a real artist at the Grand View Restaurant before.

And my father said that he should even stay and listen to the radio with us after supper because President Roosevelt was going to give a fireside chat! That did it. Franklin said he couldn't miss a chance to hear President Roosevelt. He said he's his only hope that hard times will get better and then he can make a living painting again.

So he stayed.

We had hamburger steaks with fried onions and baked beans and lettuce and tomatoes and fruit salad with cherries. Franklin helped with the dishes and then we all sat around the radio while it was raining and pouring outside and listened to the fireside chat. President Roosevelt started the way he always does: "My friends . . ." I held my breath until he started because once he forgot to say it.

My father lit up the fish tank on one side of the radio, and he explained to Franklin that he calls the fireside chats fish-tank chats because he'd love to have a fireplace but we don't so we have to settle for a fish tank.

"It *would* be nice to have a fireplace on the other side of the radio," said Franklin. "But that sure is one beautiful fish tank. And the movement of the orange goldfish is like the movement of the orange and gold flames in a fire."

Afterward, my mother said that was just like an artist to say a thing like that.

He stayed till President Roosevelt said good night. Then he said, "Thanks a lot for everything, folks. This was the best day I've had in a long time. I ate two meals in the same day and listened to FDR and felt like I had friends to talk to again."

Bang! Crash! More thunder and lightning. I thought how Skippy must be shivering in the garage and wished I could pet him.

"Listen," my father said to Franklin. "It's dark now—and it's still pouring. I've got a folding cot out in my office in the garage. Sometimes I lie down out there and take a little snooze."

"When he gets exhausted from writing those letters," said my mother.

"You and Skippy could keep each other company," said my father. "Sleep till it stops raining. Stay there all night—it's okay."

Franklin looked surprised. Then he asked my father a funny thing.

He said, "Have you got a big piece of plywood?"

My father opened the trapdoor in the bathroom and Franklin and my father and I went down the steps to the cellar. That's where my father does his hobby, carpentry, and he has wood and all his tools. He got a piece of plywood. Franklin went upstairs to measure something. Then he came back down and measured the plywood. Then he borrowed my father's saw and cut it "just the right size."

"Have you got something to keep it dry?" he asked. My father said he had a drop cloth. They wrapped it in that.

We went upstairs and Franklin thanked my mother and father again.

"I'll probably be gone when you get up," he said.

"Be sure the rain is over," said my mother.

"Good luck," said my father.

"Wait for breakfast," I said. "Maybe we could have pancakes."

Franklin smiled and took the wrapped-up piece of plywood and his knapsack and ran over to the garage. I was glad he would have a dry place to sleep and Skippy would have someone to pet him if he shivered.

I went to bed and pulled the feather quilt up over my head. I'm afraid of lightning too, like Skippy. I'm afraid of a lot of things—I'm a real scaredy-cat. But when President Roosevelt was talking and Franklin the artist was painting or talking, I forgot to be afraid.

In the morning, I ran out to the garage to see if Franklin was still out there with Skippy. But only Skippy was there. He jumped up on me and licked my face.

But on my father's desk, Edward, was: a *fireplace!*

Well, it was a *painting* of a fireplace, on the big piece of plywood. But it looked so real—there were bricks on the sides and top, sort of a rosy color, and in the middle he painted a fire!

Orange and gold to match the goldfish, he wrote in a note. *Just attach it to the wall on the other side of the radio and the next time FDR is on you'll have a fireside chat and a fish-tank chat at the same time. I left it on top of the desk so Skippy won't accidentally smear it—it needs a couple of days to dry, like the books. So long and thanks again for your kindness. I'll send you a postcard and let you know if I find work.* And he signed it, *The Other Franklin.*

My father just now attached the painted fireplace to the wall, on the other side of the radio from the fish tank. It looks *beautiful.*

So that's what's new on Route 9W, Edward. I'll bet you're sorry you asked me that question because then you had to read this whole long answer. I know you don't like reading, so you don't have to read the whole thing if you don't want to. (But ha-ha! You already did.)

Your friend,
Hannah

P.S. I can hardly wait for the next fireside chat! Do you listen to them there in Kansas too? Also, do you get men coming to your door for a sandwich or a cup of coffee and do they ask if you have any work?

THE WHITE HOUSE
1600 Pennsylvania Avenue
Washington, D.C.

April 12, 1938

Dear friend Hannah,

Thank you for your letter of April 2.

Hitch your star
To FDR

is indeed wonderful. It would have made a great slogan in my last campaign. Should the gentleman who writes rhymes one-two -three stop again at the Grand View Restaurant for one of your delicious rare hamburgers, tell him FDR appreciates the sentiment.

Mrs. Roosevelt and I also like the quote from her uncle Teddy that your mother likes: ''Keep your feet on the ground and your eyes on the stars.'' Your father and I share something in common, in that we both have a wife who is an anchor. A man who has such a wife should consider himself fortunate, as indeed I do. Sailing away into the sky like a kite would surely cramp my style.

Enclosed find an airmail stamp from another of those hard-to-spell countries (which you managed to spell correctly nonetheless): Czechoslovakia.

If you turn the stamp sideways, you will see that the design turns out to be a bird.

Warmest wishes from your friend,

Franklin D Roosevelt

Franklin Delano Roosevelt

P.S. I forgot to thank you for the compliment: ''Everybody likes you, President Roosevelt.'' It is my sad duty to report that there are many people who do not like me, my dear. In fact, there are those who dislike me so much they refuse to call me by my proper name. They refer to me instead as ''That Man in the White House.''

FDR:MAL

April 16, 1938

Dear Grandma,

President Roosevelt called me "my dear" again. The fourth time!

And he sent me a stamp from Czechoslovakia. It's a bird sideways.

And I told him everybody likes him, but he said there are some people who don't! I never heard of anybody who didn't like President Roosevelt, did you?

Yesterday I saw an advertisement for Palmolive soap in my mother's magazine, the *Woman's Home Companion.* Guess who it showed: the Dionne quintuplets! One was looking in a mirror and one was talking on the telephone and the other three were just standing around. And it said if you want a beautiful complexion like the Dionne quintuplets you should use Palmolive soap.

It made me think of when I got the measles so we couldn't see them in the movie. I'm still sorry we missed it but I'm glad we saw *Snow White.* Aunt Becky called last night and said that next time she sees me she'll tell me the whole story of the Dionne quintuplets movie. (She forgot she told me that already.) Aunt Becky's whole stories are *long.*

She said she is 60% finished with the guess-whats. I told her no hurry. But I know Aunt Becky. She'll hurry.

Love to you and Grandpa,

Hannah

April 17, 1938

Dear Hannah,

It's nice you're still writing to President Roosevelt and still getting answers. Grandpa and I like him and everybody we know likes him too. But there must be some few people who don't like him. The people who voted for that other man, Alf Landon. Luckily there are more of us. As far as I'm concerned, President Roosevelt could keep being president for the rest of my life. I would vote for him forever.

Love from Grandpa and me,
Grandma

P.S. Hannah, don't worry so much about your Aunt Becky's guess-what. After all, if you don't like it, you can hang it away in your closet and just wear it once in a blue moon when she comes to visit you. Maybe it would be a good idea if instead of worrying you could think of one good thing about Aunt Becky's knitting.

April 18, 1938

Dear Grandma,

Well, just once my aunt Becky knitted me something that even if I didn't like to wear it, it came in handy. It was a long hat called a stocking cap. It had stripes, too, red and white—like a candy cane. It was very ugly.

The day it came was after a big snow. School was called off because the buses couldn't get through. My father dug a path through the snow so our mailman, Mr. Powell, could get in. He needed two cups of coffee to warm up.

I wanted to go up to the top of the mountain to my special secret place like I always do. My mother said people with brains would stay in if they could on a day like that and I could only go out if I wore long underwear, my snowsuit, galoshes, a scarf, two pairs of gloves, and Aunt Becky's new hat. I hate long underwear. And I didn't like that hat. But I wanted to go out. It took me a long time to get dressed. I was so bundled up it was hard to bend over to put on my galoshes. I said the hat made me look dopey, but my mother said no one would see me because all the people with brains were staying inside. Even Skippy stayed inside. I guess Skippy has brains.

When I went out, I walked in the path my father made till I got to the road. I could hear icicles clicking together on the branches of the trees all the way up the Mountain Road. It sounded like a hundred Aunt Beckys with knitting needles.

When I got to the top of the mountain, to my special secret place, I looked down. I saw that the Hudson River was frozen all the way across and there was snow on it.

The ferry couldn't go. The mountain on the other side was covered with white.

Was it cold—even through all those clothes! When I started going down the mountain to go home, one of my galoshes went through the ice. It got lost in the snow underneath it. I couldn't find it! I had a bare foot and it was freezing. I couldn't walk home! So in the end I put Aunt Becky's long hat on my foot and walked down the mountain. My mother said, "Why is your hat on your foot?" and when I told her she said, "See, you never know when a thing like that could come in handy."

And Grandma, that's the only one good thing I could think of about Aunt Becky's knitting.

Love,
Hannah

April 19, 1938

Hi Hannah,

Wow! That was the longest letter I ever read!

About when you grow up and if you have a son you'll tell him he can cry. The other boys will laugh at him! They'll be like Charlie Rehnquist and those other boys on the bus. You wouldn't want that to happen, would you? Tell him it's okay to laugh or pretend to be sleeping, but don't cry. Besides, you said *you* don't cry and you're not even a boy. So how come you want your son to cry?

And about the men who come to the door for something to eat. Yes, we get them too, even though it's a long walk in from the road to our house.

My father always has plenty of work for them to do. Sometimes they help me with my chores!

Then my mother gives them a big meal because on the farm we eat big meals. It's supposed to give you energy to do all the work. Who is your Mrs. Wagner who makes pies? We give them a Mrs. Winchley pie.

I'll tell you a secret I'm not supposed to tell anybody. But you don't know anybody out here and besides I know if I ask you not to tell, you won't—right?

Guess who makes Mrs. Winchley's pies? *My father!*

My mother doesn't like to bake pies. She says she's too busy giving haircuts and permanents. She used to work in a beauty parlor before she got married so now ladies come to the house and get their hair washed, cut, and set (twenty-five cents each thing). A permanent is two dollars.

My father got the idea of the pies because he's always

trying to think of ways to earn extra money. He always worries what if we lose the farm. So all year round he delivers eggs and chickens to people's houses and in the spring, summer, and fall, we have a farm stand with fruit and vegetables. Then one day he got the idea of the pies.

My grandpa, my father's father, has the farm right next to ours. It's not our kind of a farm, though. It's a fruit orchard—peaches in the spring and summer, apples in the fall, and all kinds of other fruit in between. The blossoms start in the spring. It's very pretty and it smells good. I don't ever want to have *any* kind of a farm, but if I had to, a fruit farm is what I'd pick. No pigs, chickens, sheep, goats, or any kind of animals to get up five o'clock in the morning to feed. Except maybe one cow to keep me company: Mathilda. And her calf. To keep *her* company.

My father knows that my grandfather worries about losing his farm too. So he said to my grandfather, "How about we start a little business on the side baking pies?" Well, first he said it to my mother and she said, "Don't look at me. I've got my hands full already." That's when he asked my grandfather. I was there.

You should have heard my grandfather! He got mad! He said, "Pies? *Men* bake *pies?* Are you crazy?" When my father said he would do it anyway, my grandfather said, "Well, don't tell anybody. I don't want to be a laughing-stock. Call them Mrs. Winchley's pies." So that's what we call them.

Also my grandfather said, "Besides, who taught you to

make pies?" My father said, "Nobody yet. I'll teach myself." And he looked it up in one of my grandmother's old cookbooks that she had before she died. Then he tried it out. The first few were terrible. Once the crust was too raw. Another time it was too burned. We had to throw those out.

But then one came out just right. It was apple. The apples were from Grandpa's orchard. We ate the whole pie for dinner.

Now he mixes things together. Like apples and apricots. Rhubarb and strawberries. Cherries and walnuts. Peaches and blackberries. And boysenberries with plums. That's my favorite. He started mixing because once when he was making a peach pie, he ran out of peaches. So he filled in with blackberries. The pies are a big hit. When he delivers eggs and chickens he puts a lot of pies in back of the truck and everybody buys them. But because of what my grandfather said, we call them Mrs. Winchley's pies. So everybody says my mother is sure a good pie baker.

When a man comes to the door for something to eat and does some work to earn it, if he works really hard, my father will give him a whole pie to take with him when he goes. And before they go, my mother gives a free haircut. She says maybe just maybe they'll find a job if there is a job to find. And if they find a job they should have a good haircut.

My grandfather says they are mollycoddling those men. My father says, "*I* could be one of those men." That's why he gives them a pie.

Well, you wrote me the longest letter I ever read and now I wrote you the longest letter I ever wrote!

My teacher says I have to read another book. There is no end!

Edward

April 20, 1938

Dear President Roosevelt,

Thank you for the stamp from Czechoslovakia. I love birds. I put it in the walnut shell with the kangaroo from Australia, the giraffe from Tanganyika, the elephant from Liberia, and the bear from Switzerland.

I never heard of anybody who didn't like you, President Roosevelt.

I like you. I wrote my grandmother a letter and she said she heard of a few people who don't like you. But only a *few*. She likes you. She said she would vote for you forever if she could.

But I can tell you somebody who doesn't like *me*.

It's the delicatessen man. His name is Mr. Van Damm. He doesn't call me by my proper name either, like those people you said don't like you. He calls me "little girl." I hate that.

I see him every time I walk to the library to pick out a book.

Do you like reading, President Roosevelt? Reading is my favorite thing.

Next to my special secret place at the top of the mountain and a little cove I like down by the river, my best place to go is the library.

I walk down 9W till I get to the railroad crossing, then I'm on Cornelison Avenue. I pass Billy Allen's Tavern on the left and Van Damm's Delicatessen on the right. I always have two cents in my pocket because Van Damm's has penny candy.

When I walk in the door, a bell tinkles. Mr. or Mrs. Van Damm says, "Yes, can I help you?"

I always hope Mrs. Van Damm will wait on me because Mr. Van Damm rushes me. He is always in a hurry to get back to the kitchen, but I think *Mrs.* Van Damm is glad to get out.

I like to take my time deciding about candy. There's so much to choose from. I have a lot of favorites: gumdrops, spearmint leaves, orange slices, lemon drops, root beer barrels, licorice whips, and candy bananas. Some you get three for a penny, some two, and some just one. So choosing takes time.

But Mr. Van Damm says, "Make up your mind, little girl. I haven't got all day. I have *work* to do."

I don't like that. It makes me get mixed up. I can't choose fast.

Mrs. Van Damm lets me take my time.

She always asks me what I'm reading. She says she likes to read too.

Mr. Van Damm never asks me what I'm reading. Once when he said, "Hurry up, little girl. Stop dreaming," I got so mixed up I dropped my book. I was glad it wasn't *Heidi.* I said, "I am *not* dreaming—I'm *thinking.*" But I said it to myself, not to Mr. Van Damm. He's too grouchy.

Today Mr. Van Damm waited on me on my way to the library, so on the way home, I kept my fingers crossed so I would get *Mrs.* Van Damm. It didn't work. I opened the door, the bell tinkled, and I held my breath and looked straight into the eyes of *Mr.* Van Damm.

He gave me an awful look and you know what he said to me? He said, "What? *You* again!"

Do you think that was nice of Mr. Van Damm to say that to me, President Roosevelt?

Love from your friend,
Hannah

April 23, 1938

Dear Edward,

That *was* a long letter. And a very interesting one too.

I didn't mean I would *want* my son to cry. I just meant I don't like it when people say, "Boys can't cry." It isn't fair. And I didn't say I don't *ever* cry—I just said I don't cry in front of bullies. Because bullies *want* you to cry and I hate bullies so that's why I would never cry in front of them. Even if they tortured me! What I meant about my maybe-son is I probably would tell him not to cry around the bullies on the bus if he can help it, but otherwise if he wants to cry, he should do it.

Mrs. Wagner's pies are pies that we buy for the restaurant. We have apple, huckleberry, cherry, and coconut custard. I don't like any of them because the crust tastes like cardboard, but the customers think they're delicious.

Maybe Mrs. Wagner's pies are made by Mr. Wagner too! If so, he's a terrible baker!

When you said that about the fruit from your grandfather's orchard, it sounded nice. I would like to sit in a fruit tree in your grandfather's orchard and read a book. Do you ever do that? In fact, I wish I was sitting in a tree in your grandfather's orchard right this minute—far away from home.

Because, Edward, I am in a lot of trouble.

I did something terrible so I guess I deserve it.

I took a ride across the river on the ferryboat and I didn't get permission.

I was on top of the mountain in my special place reading

a book. I love it up there because nobody knows I'm there but me. To get in, you have to push through some very high grass. In summer, the grass is as tall as I am so I just part it with my hands when I go in and then when I let go, it closes and I'm in this private place where I can see ten miles up and down the Hudson River.

The sun was shining so much today and when it does that I just sit for a while and watch it on the water before I start my book. It sparkles all the way across to the other side. I never saw it as pretty as today. Then I saw the ferryboat. It was coming over to our side from Tarrytown. It was about halfway across.

On the ferryboat there is a man who plays the violin and holds out a tin cup and a man who comes around selling Eskimo Pies. Once we crossed the river that way when we went to see my grandmother and grandfather because New York City is on the other side, about twenty miles away. We usually go to the George Washington Bridge and cross the river that way, but once we took the ferry and it was nice. My mother and father gave me two nickels that time, one to put in the violin man's cup and one to buy an Eskimo Pie.

This time I had a quarter in my shoe that I got for a tip from a man who came to the restaurant and wrote a poem in my autograph book. It's been my lucky quarter ever since. But it wasn't so lucky today. Because all of a sudden I got an idea.

I ran down out of my secret place and down the side of the mountain and crossed Route 9W and instead of going to the restaurant, I crossed the railroad tracks and ran down to the River Road, where my other secret place is, around a little cove. I wanted to see if the river looked as pretty down there as it did from the top of the mountain. It looked even better! The sun made a shiny path straight across to Tarrytown. And over there I saw a house that looked like it had golden windows!

I looked to see if the ferry was all the way across yet. It almost was but not quite. So I thought it would be fun to have a race.

I ran up till I got to Broadway and then I ran down Broadway past the library, and down to the park. I just made it—the ferry was in. Cars drove off. Passengers got off. Then new cars got on. New passengers got on. And then I got a bad idea, but when I got it I thought it was a good idea: I took my good-luck quarter out of my shoe and followed some grown-ups who were getting on so it looked like I was with them.

Then I sat on a bench on the ferry and through a little window I watched the sun sparkle on the river all the way across. I listened to the man play the violin. He played a song we sing in Music that I like. It's called "Fleecy Clouds." I had twenty cents change left over from the quarter. So I bought an Eskimo Pie for a nickel and I put another nickel in the violin man's tin cup. Then I kept watching the sun on the water again, and when we got to the other side I went off with the passengers just long enough to touch the ground so I could say I was there. Also so I could look for the house with the golden windows. But I couldn't find it. When I turned around the golden windows were on our side!

I got back on the ferry and paid another nickel. I still had one nickel left. I gave it to the violin man because he looked poorer than the Eskimo Pie man.

On the way home I read my book a little but mostly I just watched the sun on the water through the window again. In the sky the sun started getting a little lower. The sky looked pink. It was nice.

When we got back to the park I ran home.

That's when I got in trouble.

My mother said, "Hannah Diamond, where have you been so long?"

She never calls me Hannah Diamond. So I knew she was mad.

My friend Aggie used to cross her fingers and tell her parents a little lie sometimes if she thought she was going to get in trouble. She said I should do it too, but I can't. My parents always tell me the truth so I think I have to tell them the truth too.

So I did.

I said to my mother, "I took a ride on the ferryboat."

She said, "You *what?*"

So here I am in my room. I have nothing to do but write long long letters.

I'm not allowed to go to the library or up on the mountain or down by the river for three weeks.

My favorite places in the world to be!

I might as well be in jail!

Your friend,
Hannah

P.S. And the worst thing of all is this: for the whole three weeks I'm not allowed to even walk to school. *I have to take the bus!* Ugh!

I almost forgot: I got another stamp:

April 23, 1938

Dear Grandma,

I am having a punishment!

I never had a punishment before.

Ma is so mad at me she says I have to go to my room every day after school for three weeks.

It was my own fault, what happened. But I can't think about it now.

I don't think Ma likes me just the way I am.

I'm in the doghouse is where she says I am. So at least it's good I've got Skippy to keep me company. He pushes my door open with his nose and licks my face and tries to cheer me up. Because when I can't run up the mountain and go sit in my secret place whenever I want to I really *need* cheering up.

Love to you and Grandpa,
Hannah

P.S. Do *you* still like me just the way I am?

April 25, 1938

Dear Hannah,

You know I told you I will always like you just the way you are.

When I see you, you can tell me all about it. If you want.

You have nice things you can do in your room. You can read. You can write letters to me and President Roosevelt. You can talk to your dog. You can draw.

Draw me another picture.

Love from Grandpa and me,
Grandma

April 26, 1938

Dear Mrs. Warner,

I am very sorry to tell you I will not be able to come across the street to listen to our radio program this week. Or next week or the week after. I will explain why when I see you.

I hope you will tell me all the stories of *The Witch's Tale* I am going to miss.

But if you look down from your front window at 8:30 in the morning or 3:30 in the afternoon, you can see me getting on or off the school bus. (Ugh!) We could wave to each other. Then I have to go to my room.

Love,
Hannah

P.S. Mr. Powell is delivering this free without a stamp since it is just across the street. But I am licking the envelope shut because I don't want him to know about *The Witch's Tale.*

April 27, 1938

Dear Hannah,

Wow! I'm very sorry. I hate getting in trouble. It happens to me lots of times too.

One punishment I never get though is to stay in my room. Because if I stay in my room I can't do chores! Sometimes I wish I *could* stay in my room.

When I get in trouble I go out and talk to Mathilda.

Since you have to stay in your room so long I'll try to write you more letters so you have something to read and more letters to write. (Because then you can answer me.)

The thing I get in trouble for most of the time is something really dumb.

It's because I don't talk.

Is that a thing to get in trouble for?

I hear my father ask my mother all the time, "What's the matter with that boy? Why doesn't he talk?"

My grandfather says the same thing. "Is Edward deaf and dumb?" "Well, I'm not deaf, Grandpa—I can hear that" is what I'd like to answer. Except it isn't me he's asking. It's my father. He seems to blame my father.

Once I heard my mother tell my father, "Well, you're not the world's most talkative man yourself, you know."

My teacher asked me again yesterday why I don't talk more. I told her, "I haven't got nothing to say."

You know what she said? She said, "I haven't got *anything* to say, Edward. You want to watch those double negatives." Again! Where should I watch them? I don't see them. I just say them.

Hey, Hannah, what happened to that list of double

negatives in your cubby that you said you would send me so I could learn how not to say them? This would be a good time for you to copy them down for me since you have to stay in your room and all. That way you could keep busy till your time is up and I could learn better English for when I write my book that nobody can understand to show my father. And my grandfather too.

Guess what I read for the second book the teacher said I had to read? Don't laugh. I read that one you said you like so much. *Heidi.* Even though Heidi was a girl, you said there was a boy in it too. Peter. But you know what boy I liked the best? He wasn't a boy anymore. He was a grandfather—Heidi's grandfather. I would like to have Heidi's grandfather for a grandfather. I don't think he would bother me about talking or reading—or anything.

Edward

April 27, 1938

Dear Grandma,

Here are drawings of my two favorite things inside your *chinik*. Remember I couldn't choose between the pitcher and the tiny cups that look like pineapples on a tray and the six little orange teacups? Well, first here's the pineapple pitcher:

But in the end I chose the little orange teacup with the gold around the edges even though it's not as fancy as the pineapple. I picked it because the orange looked so bright and shiny and the gold rim sparkled like the sun on the river (which I don't like to think about just now). So here's the little orange teacup:

Too bad I picked it. If I didn't it would still be there in your *chinik.*

Love to you and Grandpa,
Hannah

May 1, 1938

Dear Edward,

Thanks for writing me a long letter and sending it to me so fast so I could keep busy.

I'm sorry I never sent you that list of double negatives but when I went to do it, I couldn't. It felt mean. I threw it out.

I have a better idea: I am reading a book called *Huckleberry Finn* by Mark Twain. I only read two and a half pages and already I love it—except for one thing. There is a word Huck uses that I hate. It's a word some people use who want to hurt other people's feelings. It hurts my feelings just to look at it. I asked our librarian, Miss MacNamara, why Mark Twain uses such a terrible word. She said Mark Twain would never use that word himself, but Huck does because he learned it from his ignorant father. I'm glad I haven't got an ignorant father who would use words just to hurt other people's feelings.

But back to double negatives, here's how to learn not to use them: Just read the first two and a half pages of *Huckleberry Finn* and see if you can find the twelve double negatives yourself. *You* write them down and at the top of the page write, *Don't talk like this.* You'll learn more about how not to use double negatives from *Huckleberry Finn* than you will from anybody else! And you'll be your own teacher!

Do you have to write another book report? If so, I hope you won't have to stand up.

Your friend (still in the doghouse),
Hannah

P.S. You said you told your teacher, "I haven't got nothing to say." Well, that is one double negative I would like to comment on for a special reason: "I haven't got nothing to say" means you *have* got *something* to say. And you know what? You *do* have something to say, whether you know it or not. Every single thing you've written to me is *something* and nobody said it but you. Would I be writing all these letters to somebody who has nothing to say? I would *not*.

I have a surprise to tell you, Edward Winchley: You are an interesting person.

May 1, 1938

Dear Aggie,

You were probably wondering what GWMDTOG-TAMN stands for. So I might as well tell you. It's Girls Whose Mothers Didn't Think Of Giving Them A Middle Name. Bunny Hunnicutt and I are the only members. Because our mothers are the only ones who didn't think of it.

It was Bunny's idea so she's the president. It wasn't my idea so I'm the vice president. We didn't have an election. Bunny just said, "I'm the president." I didn't say anything.

Once a week we have a meeting and we pick a new middle name. I started with Ginger for Ginger Rogers. Another week my middle name was Shirley for Shirley Temple. Last week I was Claudette for Claudette Colbert. Like that. This week I thought I'd pick Judy for Judy Garland, but this week I can't go to a meeting. Or next week or the week after either.

I am stuck in my room for three weeks, Aggie. I crossed the river on the ferry without permission. So now I know what a punishment feels like. It's my first one.

I remember you used to get lots of punishments because your mother said cleanliness was next to godliness and your room was an unholy mess. I used to wonder how you felt when you had to stay inside so much. Now I know.

Love,
Hannah

P.S. I didn't mean *I* thought your room was an unholy mess, Aggie. I just meant that's what your mother used to say. I hope she doesn't say that anymore. And this is my sixteenth letter.

May 5, 1938

Dear Hannah,

Wow! That Huckleberry Finn speaks worse English than I do!

I am listing those double negatives in the first two and a half pages but I didn't finish yet. And I saw that word you said his ignorant father taught him. I would never say a thing like that.

I had a hard time getting that book. When I asked for it in the library, Mrs. Snapple, the librarian, said to me, "It is called *The Adventures of Huckleberry Finn,* Edward."

Huckleberry Finn, The Adventures of Huckleberry Finn—what's the difference? Some people always have to have the last word.

And *then* she said, "I believe that book will be over your head, Edward"—Why does she keep calling me Edward? Does she think I don't know my own name?—"Why don't you try *The Adventures of Tom Sawyer* instead?"

Over my head? What's that supposed to mean? Mrs. Snapple is not a person you want to mess around with so I didn't say nothing except, "I am looking up twelve double negatives in the first chapter of *Huckleberry Finn.*" (I purposely didn't say *The Adventures of. . . .*)

Was she impressed! Thanks for the idea, Hannah. She gave me *both* books.

Tom Sawyer looks easier, and I think I can read it and use it for my next book report.

Huckleberry Finn looks really hard—but I figure if your father can read that book by Albert Einstein that he says he can't understand one word of, I can read *Huckleberry Finn.* Is your father still on page nine?

I wonder if I will really ever write a book that nobody will understand one word of.

By the way, yes, I *did* have to write another book report. We do them all the time now. I wrote about *Heidi*.

This time it was easy. I just kept your letter on how to write a good book report in front of me when I was writing and I wrote all the things you said just like the last time, and guess what? I got another big red *Good!* And I didn't have no double negatives in it at all!

I did have to stand up again and read my book report. I thought maybe this time my knees and teeth wouldn't knock as much. Instead they knocked more. I don't understand it. I also don't like it. In fact I hate it.

If a person ever gets to be a genius, do you have to stand up and read things out loud? Because I don't think I'd like that very much.

Do you think my father said, "Good!" when my mother showed him the new red *Good*? Did he say, "Keep up the good work"?

No. He just said, "Keep trying, Edward."

Keep trying! What does he mean keep trying? I *am* trying. How much trying does a person have to do?

And why doesn't he ask *me* if I'd like to help him with those pies like he did my grandfather? I'd like to do that. I'd like to do the part where you take a fork and press it down all around the edges and make little lines that keep the pie shut so the juice doesn't run out. Crimping, it's called. I could also cut the *X*'s on the top. But he doesn't ask me.

Why doesn't he ask me? Because he doesn't like me, that's why.

You said something funny about staying in your room and writing a lot of long long letters. Hannah, did you ever write a short letter? I'll bet you can't. (Ha-ha, just joking.)

Edward

May 9, 1938

Dear Edward,
I'll bet I can.

Hannah
(Ha-ha, just joking too.)

P.S. "I didn't have no double negatives" is a double negative.

May 9, 1938

Dear Edward,

That wasn't a real letter I sent you earlier so it doesn't count. Here's another one.

It's about reading and a girl in my class named Edna Mae Waller and something unusual that she did today which I can't forget.

Does your teacher have different reading groups?

We have three: Bluebirds, Robins, and Chickadees.

The Bluebirds are the best readers, Robins are in the middle, and Chickadees are the worst. We're not supposed to say best, middle, and worst, we're supposed to say Bluebirds, Robins, and Chickadees. But everybody knows it just the same.

Poor Edna Mae Waller is really a Chickadee but she reads with the Bluebirds and our books are too hard for her. We sit in a circle. When it's her turn to read, sometimes she takes so long to start I think she's falling asleep. But she isn't—she's just trying to figure out what it says.

Once a terrible thing happened. Edna Mae was trying and trying to read the first sentence when it was her turn. All of a sudden she said, "I can't—I can't do it!" And she burst into tears! In front of all the other kids!

I felt terrible for Edna Mae Waller.

When I told my mother what happened, I said I wondered why Edna Mae was a Bluebird. My mother said, "Her father is a prominent person."

I said, "What's a prominent person?" and my father said, "It's a big shot."

I asked my father if he's a prominent person or a big shot because I'm a Bluebird too.

My father said, "No, I'm just an ordinary guy." He always says that.

My mother said, "There are two ways you can be a Bluebird in your school. You can be a good reader or your father can be a prominent person. You're a Bluebird because you're a good reader."

My father said it wasn't democratic for the teacher to put Edna Mae in the best reading group if she's not a good reader. He said her father being a big shot should have nothing to do with what reading group she's in.

My mother said it's not that my teacher, Miss Hopkins, is undemocratic, but Miss Valentine (the principal we had before Miss Starr, the new principal, came) probably told her to do that.

I said, "Are principals teachers' bosses? I didn't know teachers had to do what principals tell them to!"

My father said principals had a boss too. He said, "That's why I went into business for myself, even if it's just a little business. I wanted to make a living without a boss." My father likes to be his own boss.

I'd like to be a teacher when I grow up. But I'm like my father—I don't like to have a boss either.

My mother said, "It's not just that it's undemocratic for Edna Mae Waller to read with the Bluebirds when she's really a Chickadee. It's not fair to Edna Mae either. It's too hard for her so she doesn't learn to read better, and she probably worries a lot."

That's true. Once I was sitting next to Edna Mae in the

reading circle before it was her turn and she was shaking so hard! She didn't even have to stand up and she was shaking. I held her hand.

But listen to this. Today when the Bluebirds sat down in the reading circle, Edna Mae Waller didn't look down at the floor the way she usually does. She didn't shake. She didn't even wait to be called on.

She raised her hand and when Miss Hopkins said, "Yes?" Edna Mae said, "You know what? I can sing."

And she stood up, and right in front of the Bluebirds in the circle and the Robins and Chickadees at their desks, she sang!

She sang out loud.

She sang "Trees"!

Before she started, some kids were giggling.

I held my breath and crossed my fingers for Edna Mae.

But when she opened her mouth and sang, "I think that I shall never see . . ." everybody got quiet.

Edna Mae Waller has a beautiful voice!

She sang and sang. And then she sat down.

I was so happy I clapped. And then everybody else clapped too. Even Miss Hopkins. Miss Hopkins said, "Edna Mae, you *sing* like a real bluebird!"

Edna Mae couldn't stop smiling.

When I told my mother she said, "Everybody is good in some things and not in others."

Like I'm good in reading and spelling but not in arithmetic. And *you're* good in arithmetic, Edward—remember that!

Your friend,
Hannah

May 5, 1938

Dear Hannah,

That was a nice picture of the things inside the *chinik*.

You are a good artist. Maybe you could combine art with being a teacher when you grow up. You could teach the class hard words and on the blackboard you could draw pictures.

Since you can't run around up on that mountain for a while, Hannah, and I know this is hard for you, maybe you could tap-dance in your room for half an hour each day. It would be good exercise and it would help the time pass by.

Grandpa and I might try to take a day off soon to come visit you.

Love from both of us,
Grandma

P.S. And forget about that cup.

MARGUERITE "MISSY" LeHAND

May 6, 1938

Dear Hannah,

Thank you for your letters of April 10 and 12. Just around the time you were seeing that first crocus on April 12, I saw our first cherry blossoms. Washington, D.C., is quite a sight in April when the cherry trees bloom--people come from all over just to get a glimpse of them.

I was honored that you're keeping my tips on how to be a good secretary in a cubbyhole in your desk right next to President Roosevelt's stamps. I hope that someday they will be useful to you.

I'm also glad that you were pleased with my suggestion that you might want to try your hand at cartooning and was delighted to receive Copycat, which really made me laugh. I hope you'll do more.

With all best wishes,

Missy LeHand

Missy LeHand

THE WHITE HOUSE
1600 Pennsylvania Avenue
Washington, D.C.

May 7, 1938

My dear friend Hannah,

Thank you for your letter of April 20.

And thank your grandmother for the kind words.

I was sorry to hear about the person who doesn't like you. But at least he is only one person. My detractors are many, I can tell you. And perhaps he doesn't even dislike you personally but is simply tired from all his work and that makes him cross.

But no, I don't think it was nice of him to say, ''What? _You_ again!'' I can picture how I would feel if, on entering the Oval Office to greet my Cabinet, already seated at the table waiting to confer with me, one of them should look at me and say, ''What? _You_ again!'' No, I should not like that at all. In fact, I might even decide to call off the conference.

I have chosen another stamp for you. Although Newfoundland was not on your list of ten hard-to-spell countries, I am sending you this stamp nevertheless, for it is rather a handsome caribou, or reindeer, with a good-looking set of antlers, and some pine trees in the background, and I thought it might please you.

Yes, I do like reading, but if you really like

reading as much as I can see you do, you should sometime contact Mrs. Roosevelt. She is the real book lover in the White House.

Rest assured, I shall never call you ''little girl,'' my dear. I seem to recall from the distant past that I too resented being addressed as ''little boy.''

Sincere best wishes from your friend,

Franklin Delano Roosevelt

FDR:MAL

May 8, 1938

My dear niece Hannah,

The guess-whats are now 80% finished so here comes the next hint.

There are jackets, bonnets, mittens, and booties. They are all pink. I believe I told you the hint about the color already.

I thought I would bring them out in person, but Poopala-darling is still doing poorly so I am keeping her at home and when I'm finished I will mail you a big package.

You will love it.

Love and kisses,
Aunt Becky

May 11, 1938

Dear Grandma,

I'm glad you liked my pictures.

It would be wonderful if you could come out!

I tried tap-dancing around the bed, but then I got worried that if I danced up and down too much, the slats might fall out under the mattress again—the way they did when I was standing up for "The Star Spangled Banner" that time and the bed collapsed (with me in it!). Ma didn't like it so much when that happened so I don't want to do anything extra to make her mad right now. I'll wait till I get out of here and then I'll tap-dance in the living room with the player piano on again.

Aunt Becky says she's 80% finished with the guess-whats. She gave another hint besides that everything is pink. She said jackets, bonnets, mittens, booties. Bonnets, booties—what am I, a baby?

Love to you and Grandpa,
Hannah

P.S. President Roosevelt called me "my dear" again! The fifth time! And he said I should thank you for your kind words (that you like him and that you would vote for him forever).

May 13, 1938

Dear Hannah,

It's a good thing that Edna Mae Waller can sing. She sounds like me in reading. Is she good in arithmetic?

My teacher has reading groups like yours, but she doesn't call us birds. She just has A, B, and C. Guess which one I'm in.

I am almost finished with *Tom Sawyer*, which I like very much.

In fact, I like it so much, I wish I could just sit down and read it right now instead of going out to do my chores.

I hope your troubles are almost over, Hannah, so you can go up on your mountain and down by your river again.

I wish I had a mountain.

Edward

May 14, 1938

Dear Edward,

I'm out! I'm down by the river, in my secret cove. Next to me is a bunch of violets (with some wet green leaves over them to keep them from drying out).

I was just across the River Road in the little glen where I always go on Mother's Day—I used to go with Aggie to pick violets for my mother. This year on Mother's Day, I couldn't go. I made my mother a card and wrote, *Happy Mother's Day. I can't go down to pick your violets this year because I'm in prison.* She slid a note under my door: *Thanks for the card. You can pick violets when your time is up.* And she signed it *Your Mother the Warden.* I thought she'd be sorry and let me out but she didn't! When my mother says no it's no, and when she says three weeks it's three weeks.

I'm sitting here a little while to catch my breath because the place in the glen where you go to look for violets is also filled with skunk cabbage. The skunk cabbage smells so terrible you have to hold your breath. So I'm sitting here just breathing and thinking how nice it is to be out.

I brought a pad and pencil and envelope with me because I wanted to write you a thank-you note from down here. The thank-you note is for writing me all those letters while I had to stay in my room. I think that was very nice of you, Edward. How is Mathilda?

Your friend,
Hannah

P.S. I will write the rest of the letter from the mountain because you said you wish you had a mountain. So: CONTINUED in a minute!

May 14, 1938

Dear Edward,

I ran all the way up and here I am.

I got a new stamp from President Roosevelt and I brought it up here with me especially so I could sit on the mountain and trace it for you.

I wish you had a mountain to sit on too. I love it up here.

Your friend,
Hannah

P.S. After three weeks riding on the bus again, I decided it was even worse than I remembered it. That big bully Marty Clark has a new thing now besides making Lottie Biddle and Joseph Spratt cry. When the bus gets near the school he yells, "Last one off is a rotten egg." Then everybody has a stampede and knocks each other down trying to get off the bus first because nobody wants to be the rotten egg. I think Marty Clark is the rotten egg if you ask me. But nobody asks me.

Hannah Diamond
Route 9W
Grand View, New York

Mrs. Eleanor Roosevelt
The White House
1600 Pennsylvania Avenue
Washington, D.C.

May 14, 1938

Dear Mrs. Roosevelt,

My name is Hannah Diamond and I am writing to you because President Roosevelt says you are the real book lover in the White House.

I love reading better than anything in the world. So I wanted to write you a letter.

I am writing from the most beautiful place I ever saw: It's a special secret place I have on top of a mountain and I love to sit here and look down at the Hudson River and read.

I especially like it if it's a nice sunny day like today so I can watch the sun sparkle on the water.

Lately I got in trouble for trying to follow the sun across the river, but I won't tell about that now except to say I did something I wasn't supposed to do without permission.

I just got out of my room where I had to stay for three weeks and I was so happy to be out I first ran down to a glen by the River Road and picked violets for my mother under a lot of skunk cabbage, which smelled so terrible I had to hold my breath, and then I ran up the Mountain Road the fastest I ever ran. And here I am sitting in the sun and writing to you.

I was wondering who is your favorite author and if you always liked to read. Did you read a lot when you were in school like me or just in the White House?

My mother reads your column, "My Day." She thinks it's wonderful and she cuts them out and pastes them in a scrapbook. She reads some out loud to my father and me. We think it's wonderful too.

When I read about your day, it makes me wish I could write about my day sometimes too, except I don't do anything except write letters to my best friend, Aggie Branagan, who moved and promised to be my pen pal but doesn't even answer me even though I wrote sixteen letters already!

My mother says you should be the next president.

She says you're very very busy doing good things all over the world and I shouldn't pester you. I wrote to President Roosevelt and Miss Missy too so my mother says now I am pestering the whole White House (and also using up too many three-cent stamps).

Am I pestering you, Mrs. Roosevelt? If I am, I'm sorry. But if I'm not, maybe you would have time to answer me someday.

Your friend,
Hannah Diamond

P.S. When you were my age, did you ever do things you were not supposed to do without permission?

May 14, 1938

Dear Grandma,

I was up on the mountain—my first day out! When I got home, there was a package for me from Aunt Becky! I hated to open it, but Ma made me. Wait till you hear what was inside!

It was a little cardboard suitcase with a knitted jacket—lumpy, bumpy, and pink.

An envelope was taped to the jacket. It said READ THIS FIRST.

Inside it said:

> Dear Hannah,
>
> Surprise!
>
> This is your consolation prize because you missed the movie of the Dionne quintuplets when you got the measles.
>
> Don't faint!
>
> Love,
> Aunt Becky
>
> P.S. What should I knit next?

I said what I always say: "Please knit nothing next." I didn't say it out loud though because Ma was watching.

She said, "Hannah, what are you waiting for? Take off the jacket and look inside."

I hate to try on woolly itchy knitted things, so I took as long as I could. I took off the jacket. I opened the snaps on the suitcase. I held my breath. And I looked inside.

What a surprise! I almost *did* faint!

It was the *Dionne quintuplets!* Marie, Annette, Cecile, Yvonne, and Emilie!

Five tiny dolls, all dressed up in pink! Pink bonnets, pink jackets, pink leggings, pink booties. All wool and full of lumps and bumps—and I don't care. I love them all.

I worried for nothing—the clothes were for *them,* not for me!

For the first time, I rushed to write Aunt Becky a thank-you note before my mother even told me to.

I wrote:

> Dear Aunt Becky,
>
> Thank you for the consolation prize. It's the best present of my life.
>
> Love,
> Hannah

And for the first time I answered her P.S. I knew just what to say. I said:

> P.S. About what to knit next, Aunt Becky. Surprise me! Knit five.

Well, Grandma, I have to go now. I'm bringing the quintuplet dolls across the street to show Mrs. Warner. It isn't the day for our radio program but I can't wait. I'll bring them again on the radio day and the seven of us can all listen together.

Too bad my friend Aggie Branagan who doesn't answer my letters and be my pen pal isn't here. She would love those quintuplet dolls as much as I do.

Love to you and Grandpa,
Hannah

P.S. Tomorrow is a meeting of the GWMDTOGTAMN Club. I'll bring the quintuplet dolls to show Bunny. I can't wait till she asks me what my new middle name is. You know how Aggie Branagan has two middle names: Agnes Maria Theresa? I'll have *five*: Hannah Marie Annette Cecile Yvonne Emilie. I'll bet nobody in the world has more middle names than that!

May 16, 1938

Dear Hannah,

What a wonderful surprise from your aunt Becky!

See—it shows you something: You should always keep an open mind.

People can turn around and do something wonderful you never expected.

It's almost better than seeing the movie!

How about drawing me a picture so I can see them too?

Love from Grandpa and me,

Grandma

May 18, 1938

Dear Grandma,

This is how it looks when the little cardboard suitcase is open.

Each doll has a separate place to stay. They are *so* cute. I take them with me everyplace I go.

I didn't draw the lumps and bumps on the knitted clothes. First, I don't know how. Second, I wouldn't even if I could. I'm like you: I like them just the way they are!

Love to you and Grandpa,
Hannah
(and Marie, Annette, Cecile,
Yvonne, and Emilie)

ELEANOR ROOSEVELT

May 20, 1938

Dear Hannah,

Tell your mother that correspondence between one book lover and another is never pestering. Besides, I remember how it feels to be young and lonely.

I pester President Roosevelt all the time: We keep an ''Eleanor basket'' on the night table next to his bed, into which I drop notes, memos, or letters, with my suggestions or ideas that I think he should take into consideration. He calls me ''my missus,'' and I wouldn't be surprised if he secretly thinks of the Eleanor basket as ''my missus' pester basket,'' though he is too polite to say so.

I have an idea about how you might save on stamps: If you have a note for the president or Missy, just drop it into a letter to me--fold it up with the name of who it's for, and I won't peek because I'm a big believer in privacy--and I'll drop it into the Eleanor basket. Thus you'll be able to write to any or all of us for the same three cents.

Now, about your questions. I should like to answer your last one first: When I was your age, did I ever do things I was not supposed to do without permission?

The answer is a resounding yes! I sat up in a

cherry tree without telling anyone I was there, and I read books I was not supposed to read (and stuffed myself with cherries). I hid books (again books I was not supposed to read) under my mattress and took them out and read them at hours when I was not supposed to be reading but sleeping. I read everything I wanted to whether I had permission or not. So now you also have the answer to your question, Did I always like to read or did I wait till I got to the White House?

Now, without asking what it was that got you into trouble, knowing only that you tried to follow the sun across the water, I can answer a third question: My favorite writer is a poet, Emily Dickinson, and I'm sure that she could appreciate your predicament about the sun. Consider the following lines she wrote:

> I'll tell you how the sun rose--
> A ribbon at a time.
> The steeples swam in amethyst,
> The news like squirrels ran.
>
> The hills untied their bonnets,
> The bobolinks begun.
> Then I said softly to myself,
> ''That must have been the sun!''

This is a poem I am particularly fond of. I hope it pleases you as well.

How lovely it sounds to have a special secret place at the top of a mountain where you can look down at the river and read. Did you know that President Roosevelt and I once lived along that same beautiful Hudson River when we were your age—I with my grandmother in Tivoli, New York, after my parents died, and President Roosevelt with his parents in nearby Hyde Park? (Did you know also, incidentally, that he and I are cousins so that my name was already Roosevelt before it became, once again, Roosevelt?)

I am sorry to hear about your friend who hasn't responded to your sixteen letters. I would keep right on writing—and I would forget about the numbers! People like you and me who love to read usually also love to write, but there are others who couldn't answer a letter if their lives depended on it. I would wager that your friend enjoys hearing news of her old school and her old friend. Of course it is nicer to receive an answer, but when I don't get one, if it's a friend I really care for, I keep on writing anyway. Of course, on the other hand, if I decide that this friend and I no longer have anything to say to each other, then that is another story.

Thank your mother and father for the compliments about ''My Day.''

Best wishes from a fellow book lover,

Eleanor Roosevelt

Eleanor Roosevelt

P.S. Enclosed is a small blank book in which you can write your own ''My Day.'' Anyone can, you know. It isn't necessary to go all over the world; all sorts of things happen right in one's own backyard. Since this is for your own personal perusal, feel free to write anything you want. No one will see it but you!

By the way, my favorite flower is the violet! And about having to poke through the strong-smelling skunk cabbage before you could find the violets, it strikes me that that is a lot like life: half violets (which delight us with their beauty and their color) and half skunk cabbage (which smells). The thing to do is to focus on the violets!

My Day

by Hannah

Today when I got home from school, my father called me down to the cellar to paint something on a sign he made. He said it was a surprise. I heard him banging and hammering down there a lot while I was in my room for that punishment I got, so I knew he was making something, but he didn't finish till today.

It was a new sign. He always cuts all the letters out of wood, which takes a long time, and then I get to paint either some of the letters or the punctuation. This time he had painted all the letters himself. Here's what it said: KEEP YOUR FEET ON THE GROUND AND YOUR EYES ON THE STARS.

"That's the saying Ma liked so much from President Teddy Roosevelt," I said. "But no fair! You didn't leave me anything to paint."

"I *did,*" he said. "That's the surprise."

He took a long thin piece of wood that he had sandpapered so it was very smooth. Then he placed it under one of the words. The word was GROUND. He used tiny little nails to hammer it in. He let me hammer two of the nails. And then he let me paint the whole line. I even got to pick the color—red. I painted very carefully with a thin brush he gave me so none of the red would get on the background of the sign, which is white. When I finished, it looked glossy and good.

"I made this for you and your mother both," he said. "She'll be happy because it's a promise to keep my feet on the ground and only my eyes on the stars."

"What about me?" I asked. "What'll I be happy about?"
"Yours is just a reminder," he said.
"Reminder of what?" I asked. "I don't get it."
"Stay off the water," he said.
I got it.

May 16, 1938

Dear Folks,

Hello from the other Franklin—in Oregon! Remember I said I'd write and let you know if I found a job? Well, I did! I'm a logger in a logging camp. We go into the forest and cut down trees. The job is through the WPA, which President Roosevelt made to help unemployed people.

We get up early and work hard all day long, but the trees smell delicious and when I look up, I can see the sky through the spaces between the branches.

We each get a cot to sleep on, all in a row, and three meals a day and not much money but enough for me to buy a sketch pad and colored pencils. In my spare time, which there isn't much of, I draw the trees. And the other loggers. I still think of you and remember the wonderful day I spent with you at the Grand View Restaurant.

Hannah, see other postcard.

Franklin Elliot

May 16, 1938

Dear Hannah,

I remember that you did a good drawing of goldfish when I stopped at the Grand View Restaurant. We artists have to stick together so here's a rough sketch I made just for you of the trees and the loggers. I think trees are very beautiful. Did you know, by the way, that paper is made from trees?

Oregon is very beautiful too—if you don't mind rain.

The Other Franklin

May 22, 1938

Dear Franklin,

We got your postcards! We are very happy you found a job.

Thanks for the extra postcard with the drawing. Mr. Powell, the mailman, liked the picture too. He doesn't read our letters because they're sealed but he does read our postcards. Thanks for calling me an artist and saying artists should stick together. I like sticking together. I had a best friend, Aggie Branagan, and we used to stick together but then she moved and promised to be my pen pal but she isn't. I guess she got unstuck.

You said you think trees are beautiful and smell delicious. I do too!

When I walk up to my special secret place at the top of the mountain, where I'm writing to you from now, that's what I look at all the way up: the trees.

Love from your friend who wishes
she knew where to send this,
Hannah

P.S. I don't mind rain. I don't like thunder and lightning like we had when you were here, but I love just plain rain. I like to hear it when I'm in bed the best. One day when I had to stay in my room I wrote a poem about it. My mother said I should show it to my teacher but I didn't. Maybe I'll send it to Mrs. Roosevelt instead. She likes poems and she sent me one by a real poet, Emily Dickinson.

My Day

by Hannah

Whew! What a night! It's back to *The Witch's Tale* at last and this was the best one yet!

Mrs. Warner is giving me knitting lessons, starting one hour before the program. She loves the quintuplet dolls, but she doesn't love the things Aunt Becky knitted for them because of the lumps and bumps. She wanted to unravel everything and start over. I asked her not to. I told her what my mother said about it's the thought that counts and how I like them just the way they are. So we're knitting new things instead.

She's knitting capes. I'm knitting scarves. She says straight things are easiest to start with. She taught me cast on and cast off and count stitches. She taught me knit one, purl two. She bought a big skein of pink wool and said, "Hold out your arms" and looped it this way and that into a big pink ball. She gave me my own pair of knitting needles!

I now bring Marie, Annette, Cecile, Yvonne, and Emilie everyplace I go. Right along with my Crayolas, my sketch pad, and *Heidi.*

I brought them to my secret place at the top of the mountain.

I brought them down to the little cove I like down by the river.

And now I brought them back to Mrs. Warner's.

I was glad we started early because I didn't think I could

knit and listen to the radio at the same time, especially since I am just learning knit one, purl two.

Mrs. Warner knits right through *The Witch's Tale.* She knits big sweaters for her two grown-up sons who don't come to visit often enough. Her needles click away just like Aunt Becky's, but her knitting comes out smoother. She never makes a mistake. She never skips a stitch. She says she's probably the world's most perfect knitter. So I'm lucky she's giving me lessons.

She showed me which way was knit and which way was purl. On knit one, the knitting needle goes over the other, and on purl, it goes *under* the other. It's fun.

But when we listened to *The Witch's Tale,* I got so excited I forgot which way was knit and which was purl.

I forgot *everything.* I'll have to start over again next week because when we listened I got so excited I dropped my needles. I didn't want Mrs. Warner to see so I didn't tell her. I didn't want her to think I'm a scaredy-cat. I don't like *anybody* to think I'm a scaredy-cat.

The reason is I *am* a scaredy-cat. But I don't want anybody to know. Well, except Edward maybe.

Now back to *The Witch's Tale.*

Tonight was the best.

There was this lady and she had a boyfriend. The problem was that she was married!

Her boyfriend was poor but kind. Her husband was rich but mean.

The lady and her boyfriend had a date in a castle at the top of a mountain with a five thousand two hundred and eighty foot drop to the bottom!

"That's high up!" Mrs. Warner said.

"It's exactly a mile," I told her.

"You're a smart girl," said Mrs. Warner. I didn't tell her my teacher Miss Hopkins told us that.

The husband found out! He drove up the winding road to the castle. Mrs. Warner and I were winding balls of wool.

Nobody knew the castle was there except the three of *them* because it was a secret castle he built for *her* when he first got rich but before he got mean. He was so rich he owned the whole mountain, including the road. The sign at the bottom said PRIVATE ROAD. NO TRESPASSING. The announcer said so.

"Look out! He's coming!" I almost screamed. They were *kissing!*

The husband parked the car and went to the door.

Would they hear me there in that castle if I screamed? And what would Mrs. Warner think? Maybe she wouldn't invite me to listen with her anymore. Maybe the invitation would be wiped out, like that poor boyfriend was going to be in a few seconds, only he didn't know it yet. *I* knew it. I didn't scream but that's when I dropped my knitting.

The husband found them.

He shot the boyfriend—with a gun!—and *Mrs. Warner* screamed!

The lady said, "Kill me too!" But he said, "No—killing's too good for you! I'm leaving you here in the castle, alone together—forever! Nice and cozy the way you wanted to be."

"But he's dead," she said.

"I know," he said.

"He ought to know!" said Mrs. Warner. "He's the murderer!"

"I hate him!" I said.

He cut the telephone wires.

He locked them in.

He threw away the key!

And the only way out was the window—to the rocky cliffs, five thousand two hundred and eighty feet below!

He drove down the mountain, around and around the winding road. My yarn was unraveled all over the floor.

The lady screamed! And screamed and screamed and *screamed!*

But there was nobody to hear her. . . .

Except Mrs. Warner, Marie, Annette, Cecile, Yvonne, Emilie, and me.

Click! Mrs. Warner turned the radio off. "Wasn't that lovely?" she said. She made Postum and brought out the cookies. I rewound the pink into balls. I only drank half my Postum and had just one cookie.

Then I said, "Thank you for a very nice evening," the way my mother says I should. Mrs. Warner stacked the cups and saucers. I put the dolls and wool and knitting needles into the suitcase and ran down the long steep stairway to the road. I took two steps at a time. I could hear the dolls' heads clacking together.

It's right across the street, I told myself. *Just don't look around!*

The moonlight made the road so white it looked like snow. I ran so fast I crashed right into the front door of the Grand View Restaurant.

My father came to the door. "What's the matter?" he asked. "You're all out of breath. Stop and inhale some of this nice fresh air with me."

"Too tired," I said.

"Well," said my mother when I came in, "did you have a nice quiet evening with Mrs. Warner?"

"Yes," I said. I crossed my fingers so it wouldn't be a lie. "I have to go to bed now."

I ran into my bedroom and put Marie, Annette, Cecile, Yvonne, and Emilie on the pillow next to mine. I took off my shoes, jumped into bed with all my clothes on, and pulled the feather quilt up to my nose.

I put my pillow over my head so I wouldn't hear the lady screaming in the castle. But I heard her *inside* my head.

So I took the pillow off and got my flashlight, and I've got the covers over me like a tent now and I'm writing it all down.

I never heard such a scary story in my whole life! It was terrible!

I can't wait for next week!

May 23, 1938

Dear Mrs. Roosevelt,

Thank you for the letter and the poem and the book. I loved them all.

I was very glad that when you were my age you did things you weren't supposed to do without permission too.

I wrote a poem and here it is:

About Rain

I like the sound the rain makes,
Especially at night,
When I am safe inside my bed,
All tucked in nice and tight.
I like it when the rain bangs hard
And smacks down like it's mad.
I like it when the rain turns soft
And whispers like it's sad.
And when there's just the puddles left—
That's raindrops in a heap—
Why, then I like to close my eyes,
Curl up, and go to sleep.

I am sending it to you because if I show it to my teacher she'll make me stand up in front of the class and read it. I don't like to do that.

You stand up and talk in front of people and even make speeches! I see you on the newsreels when I go to the movies. I could never do that!

Love from your friend,
Hannah

May 23, 1938

To Bunny Hunnicutt
President of the GWMDTOGTAMN Club

Dear Bunny,

I am very sorry to tell you I am resigning from the club.

I now have not just one but five middle names that I am not going to change anymore. So there will not be anything left for me to do at the meetings.

Love,
Hannah Marie Annette Cecile Yvonne Emilie Diamond
Vice President

P.S. And another thing: When you became the president, we did not have an election. That was undemocratic.

May 23, 1938

Dear Aggie,

You would probably like to know I resigned from the GWMDTOGTAMN Club.

I couldn't tell Bunny Hunnicutt the real reason because it would hurt her feelings. The real reason was Bunny Hunnicutt is very boring. She should change the name of her club to the IWBYTD Club. (I Will Bore You To Death Club.) See, I was looking for a new friend, but I'd rather be alone than be bored to death.

When you were my friend, you were never boring.

Guess what? I am not going to number my letters anymore. I decided to keep writing to you without counting even though you never answer. Isn't that a good idea? (I'd like to say it was *my* good idea but it wasn't. It was Mrs. Roosevelt's.)

Because I *like* writing letters.

And you are still Aggie who was my friend for a long long time.

Love,
Hannah

ELEANOR ROOSEVELT

May 30, 1938

Dear Hannah,

I liked your poem ''About Rain.'' I can understand your not wanting to stand up in front of your class and read it aloud, though. When I was your age I hated to get up and speak too.

Actually I have always disliked public speaking, believe it or not. But there came a time when I realized I had to do it to help President Roosevelt and help the country during these hard times. So I made myself a motto: ''You must do the thing you think you cannot do.'' For I knew the reason I hated it was that I was afraid of it. Now every time I make myself do something I am afraid to do, afterward I feel a bit better for it. In fact, sometimes I feel like a hero, for I say to myself, I thought I could not do it and I did it anyhow!

But I do want you to know that I understand how you feel.

Here's another poem by Emily Dickinson, who, incidentally, never stood up and read out loud but just stayed inside her house in Amherst, Massachusetts, and wrote gems like this for us to read. (I read it when I was young and felt she was talking straight to me!)

I'm nobody! Who are you?
Are you nobody, too?

Then there's a pair of us—don't tell!
They'd banish us, you know.

How dreary to be somebody!
How public, like a frog
To tell one's name the livelong day
To an admiring bog!

I'm hoping you will write more poetry whether you read it out loud or not.

Love from your friend,

Eleanor Roosevelt

June 3, 1938

Dear Edward,

Mrs. Roosevelt says, "You must do the thing you think you cannot do." I was thinking: What is the thing I think I cannot do? It's to tell Marty Clark to shut up—on the bus. Marty Clark is just like your Charlie Rehnquist. All bullies are alike. They need somebody like Mrs. Roosevelt's uncle Teddy to speak softly and carry a big stick. Somebody should tell them to shut up. I'd like to tell Marty Clark to shut up, but because I'm a scaredy-cat all I do is look out the window. If I told Marty Clark to shut up, would you tell Charlie Rehnquist to shut up? We could pick a day. We could tell them to shut up on the same day. June 15 would be good. Then I would write to you and tell you what happened and you could write to me and tell me what happened. Mrs. Roosevelt says you feel like a hero sometimes after you do the thing you think you cannot do.

I'd like to feel like a hero just once in my life.

Your friend,
Hannah

My Day

by Hannah

Today, after school, I went roller-skating down the little hill on the River Road all by myself. I haven't done that since Aggie moved. We always had a race and we both fell down at the bottom. Today I fell down by myself which wasn't as much fun because there wasn't anybody to laugh with. Falling by yourself isn't funny. I scraped my knee.

But it was worth it. Because on the ground I saw something so pretty. It wasn't on the sidewalk. It was in the road *next* to the sidewalk.

It was a puddle with a rainbow in it! It had all those colors like the colors on a pigeon's neck—pink, lavender, and green, all silvery and shiny. These colors were the same! And all inside a puddle. It smelled a little, but not as bad as the skunk cabbage in the woods. And it was still beautiful.

If I hadn't fallen down, maybe I wouldn't have seen the colors.

When I went home, I told my mother and father. My father said what I smelled was gasoline from a car that dripped into that puddle! Gasoline and water don't mix, he said. But they can make a rainbow.

There are so many unusual things in the world—you can get a surprise every day!

June 4, 1938

Dear Mrs. Roosevelt,
I loved "I'm Nobody!"
I wrote another poem. Here it is:

Colors

Colors, colors!
Rings of colors:
in a gasoline puddle,
on a pigeon's neck,
on a grackle's back.
Looking for colors:
down deep, deep down
in this cool dark place
under the skunk cabbage—
hold your breath—
until you get to
the violets.

I drew the violet for you because you said it's your favorite flower. I like having the same favorite flower as you.

Love,
Hannah

P.S. I made another comic strip for Miss Missy, and I'm putting it in here because you said you would put it in the Eleanor basket so I could save a stamp. It's okay for you to look too.

June 5, 1938

Dear Miss Missy,

I'm glad you liked the first *Copycat.* Here is the second. I hope this one makes you laugh too:

I asked Mrs. Roosevelt to put this in the Eleanor basket next to President Roosevelt so he could give it to you and I could save three cents.

Love from your friend,
Hannah

P.S.

June 7, 1938

Dear Hannah,

I'm not a good reader and I don't talk and when I do talk I say double negatives. But I'm not crazy! If I told Charlie Rehnquist to shut up on the bus, he'd knock my block off. Charlie Rehnquist is twice as big as I am. He'd say, "You wanna fight, Winchley?" I don't like to fight. But I don't want *him* to know that. You're a girl so you can do it. Marty Clark is not going to hit a girl. So I'll just keep on pretending I'm asleep on my bus and you can say shut up on your bus. Tell me what happens. Good luck. When I pretend I'm asleep on June 15, I'll keep my fingers crossed for you.

And you keep your fingers crossed for Mathilda. Because that is the day the calf is supposed to get born.

Edward

P.S. What is speak softly and carry a big stick and who is Mrs. Roosevelt's uncle Teddy?

June 11, 1938

Dear Edward,

Mrs. Roosevelt's uncle Teddy was President Theodore Roosevelt. He was president before we were born. He had a lot of sayings. One of them was "Speak softly and carry a big stick."

I think what it means is you don't have to yell or anything, just keep your voice soft—like the way you speak to Mathilda, Edward. At the same time, look a bully straight in the eye and let him know you mean business. Like if speaking softly doesn't work, you might bop him one with a big stick or something.

That's what I think it means anyway.

Your friend,
Hannah

P.S. I'll be thinking of Mathilda on June 15 too. I hope she has a nice little calf. I wish I could see it!

My Day

by Hannah

I was walking to the library. On the way I peeked in the window at Billy Allen's Tavern. I wished I could go inside to see the big picture of Madame Chiang Kai-shek over the bar, but my mother says ladies don't go to bars. I don't know why not. There's a sign right on the window. It says LADIES INVITED.

I was standing there just wishing.

I heard some noise from across the street. I turned around and saw it came from Van Damm's Delicatessen. The front door flew open. A big bowl of something came flying out. It looked like potato salad. It fell on the ground and the bowl smashed all over the sidewalk. I heard, "I hate you, you S.O.B.!" Loud! And who came flying out the door right after the potato salad but Mrs. Van Damm!

She ran across the street. She stood right next to me at the door of Billy Allen's. She recognized me and her face got all red. She put her hands over my ears. She said, "You didn't hear that!" Then she ran inside Billy Allen's. She left the door open. So I ran in after her.

It was dark in there like my mother said it would be. It smelled smoky. There was sawdust on the floor.

Madame Chiang Kai-shek was over the bar twice as big as a real person. She looked scary.

Mrs. Van Damm sat down in a booth. I sat next to her. She bought me a root beer.

"Listen, I lost my head," she said. "Sometimes people do that. Please don't tell anybody what I said."

I promised. I never tell on people. Because I wouldn't like people telling on me.

Also I like Mrs. Van Damm.

"You're the one who likes books, like I do," she said. "We understand each other."

She hates him, I said to myself.

So I said to her, "I hate him too."

She started to cry!

"No," she said. "I don't really hate him. I just hate working together all day long seven days a week three hundred sixty-five days a year. And he can be so bossy."

I told her sometimes when a bus comes and my mother tells my father to put up the sign NO BUSES and he doesn't and all the people jump off the bus and make noise and steal stuff off the front counter and wreck the place, sometimes my mother walks away and down Route 9W till she cools off. Then in the end she turns around and comes back and helps my father clean up the mess.

"Yes, it's like that," she said. "And I'm sorry you saw what you saw and heard what you heard. Never repeat it. It's not a nice way to talk."

I promised I would never repeat it.

I asked her if she'd like to walk to the library with me, but she said no, it was time to go back and help him clean up.

I gave Madame Chiang Kai-shek one last look while Mrs. Van Damm paid, and then we went out the door together. Mr. Van Damm was out in the street hosing down the gutter. He looked at me and gave me a dirty look. I gave him a dirty look right back. Then she squeezed my hand and said good-bye. "Thank you," she said. "You helped me by listening and talking." I squeezed her hand right back. Like Edna Mae Waller.

I thanked her for the root beer. Then she crossed the street to Mr. Bossy and I walked down to Broadway and went to the library.

In her "My Day," Mrs. Roosevelt does wonderful things and helps lots and lots of people. I'd like to do that too, but I don't know how. But Mrs. Van Damm said I helped her by just listening and talking. So I helped *one* person.

And that was *my* day.

I still hate Mr. Van Damm.

June 15, 1938

Dear Hannah,

What happened on the bus? Did you do it? Did you say shut up? Did you walk softly and carry a big stick or what?

I didn't even get to go to school today so I wasn't on our bus. Because when I went out at five A.M. to do my chores, Mathilda was lying down and I saw her calf was getting ready to be born. Because from the outside of Mathilda, you could see the calf was moving around *inside* Mathilda—I mean, her skin was moving, sort of with a same rhythm, swirling round and round. She didn't moan; she didn't moo. She just made a kind of a soft sound also with a kind of a rhythm to it.

So I called my father and guess what: I got to help deliver the calf! We didn't have to call the vet so my father said I saved him money. Guess what he said to me? He said, "Well done."

Tonight he let me crimp one of Mrs. Winchley's pie crusts.

And he let me pick the name for the calf.

Guess what I named her, Hannah?

I named her Hannah!

Edward

P.S. *What happened on the bus?*

June 19, 1938

Dear Edward,

I am so excited about the calf! I never had a calf named after me before! I still wish I could see her.

About the bus—well, I tried to walk softly and carry a big stick but everything went wrong.

When Marty Clark started saying, "Spratt, Spratt, the scaredy-cat" and "Bawl Baby Biddle" and they started crying, I said softly, "You shut up, Marty Clark." He heard me and just laughed. He said, "What did you say, Miss Pip-squeak?"

I jumped up. I forgot to speak softly. I said *loud*, "You shut up, Marty Clark!" He just laughed and called me Miss Pip-squeak again.

Then I lost my head. I yelled, "SHUT UP, YOU S.O.B.!"

He stopped laughing. The bus got quiet.

I was so mad about pip-squeak, I wanted to give him a big stick. But I didn't have one—so I used my foot. I gave him a kick in the shins. He fell down and hit his nose and got a nosebleed!

Edward—I got all mixed up and did everything wrong, and I am back in my room again! And I *don't* feel like a hero. I feel like a pip-squeak.

Your friend,
Hannah

P.S. But having a calf named after me makes up for it.

June 19, 1938

Dear Mrs. Van Damm,

I am very sorry to tell you I broke my promise never to say S.O.B.

I got mad at a boy on the bus and I lost my head.

I did not mean to say it. I just meant to say shut up, but I got mad at a bully. I hate bullies.

If a person breaks a promise, I know you should make up for it. The only way I can think of to make up for it is to tell you I did it and to promise not to do it again. Maybe this time I should just promise to *try* not to do it again. I will also try not to lose my head again.

I would tell you this in person, but I'm not allowed out of my room this week.

Did you read any good books lately?

Your friend,
Hannah

June 19, 1938

Dear Grandma,

It was very nice of you and Grandpa to close up the store for a day to come to see me.

My mother told me you put a sign on your door: CLOSED DUE TO EMERGENCY IN FAMILY.

I was so happy to see you both and to have you keep me company, but really, Grandma, I am not an emergency.

And I did *not* punch that boy in the nose. I couldn't even *reach* his nose if I tried. What I did was I kicked him in his shins. He fell on his nose. Can I help it if he is clumsy? Can I help it if he has more blood in his nose than anybody I ever heard of? *No.*

But *he* can help it that he is a bully. He bullies everybody on the bus. I couldn't stand it anymore is why I did it.

You know what? I'm not even going to ask you if you still like me just the way I am. *Because I know you do!*

It was fun playing school with you in my room, Grandma.

And thank Grandpa for bringing me the *two* charlotte russes.

I really *am* lucky having a grandma and grandpa like you!

Love,
Hannah

P.S. Mrs. Warner said to thank you for the delicious matzo ball soup.

June 23, 1938

Dear Hannah,

You should better have pretended to be asleep on the bus like I thought I would do before I had to stay home and help with the birthing.

But I guess you have to do things your way and I have to do things my way.

I am very sorry for what happened to you.

I am *so* sorry that I am sending you something I was trying to get up nerve to send you for quite a while.

What happened was I picked a twig off a branch on one of the trees in my grandfather's apple orchard when the buds came out. They're usually out in May but this year they were very late because we had that frost the end of April that I told you about. I picked it to send you for a present. But I never sent anybody a present before and I didn't know what to say.

So while I was thinking what to say, I wrapped it in wet paper towels, tight, so no air could get in, and I put it in a corner in a special hiding place behind the ice in our icebox. I'm the one who puts in new ice every day so I took good care of it and made sure it didn't get squashed.

Then I wrapped it in the silver foil I save from chewing gum wrappers. And I put it in this box. I had money saved up for airmail stamps so it would get there fast with this letter.

If you put the twig in a glass of water and watch, soon the bud will open into a blossom. I know you hate to be inside when you could be outside, so a blossom might make you feel a little bit like you *are* outside.

I just decided what to say! I'm sending it because I *want* to!

Edward

P.S. About what you did, Hannah? I took your letter out to the barn and read the whole thing to Mathilda and Hannah Junior (that's what I am calling her). They listened nice and quietly, just like when I read a book report. I think you *were* a hero. So far in my life I was never a hero.

June 20, 1938

Dear Folks,

I got a better job with the WPA! I am painting again!

My boss at the logger's camp saw my sketch of the trees and showed it to someone in charge of a program I didn't even know existed: There is a special program for artists! We paint murals in libraries, hospitals, schools, post offices, wherever we are asked to do it.

My boss is a lady. I think she's the best artist I ever met; she thinks I am. So naturally we get along fine.

Why I am writing to tell you this, aside from the fact that I promised to let you know how I was coming along, is I want to tell you about our latest job. It's a mural in a library—still in Oregon.

Too bad Grand View is so far away from here or you could come and see it. The best I can do is tell you about it and send you a sketch:

There is a garden.

In this garden is one tree.

The tree is covered with so many birds you can't even see what kind of a tree it is—it looks like a bird tree!

The birds are goldfinches. My boss, a bird-watcher, told me a bunch of goldfinches is called a *charm* of goldfinches—isn't that nice?

All around the rest of the garden roses are growing. But something else is growing between the roses, and that is books!

It is a garden of roses and birds and *books!* And children.

A sign on the fence says COME IN AND PICK YOUR OWN BOOKS.

The children are picking the books out of the bushes! Now find one girl sitting in the tree, pulling a book out of the top of a bush. There is a dog below her. Look at the girl and look at the dog and look at the title of the book. I think you will get a surprise.

Remember, this is just a sketch. I wish you could see it in person so you could see the colors.

Thanks again for everything,
Franklin Elliot
(the *other* Franklin)

P.S. As soon as I have a permanent address I'll send it to you.

June 25, 1938

Dear Edward,

I think helping deliver a calf is being a hero.

But listen, I want to tell you something:

You don't have to be a hero.

You don't have to be Albert Einstein.

Just be Edward Winchley.

I like you just the way you are.

I think you are the nicest boy I never met.

Your friend,
Hannah

P.S. I saved the best for last: the bud! It blossomed—overnight. It's beautiful! It's in a glass of water on my desk. I think a present somebody sends you just because he wanted to is the best thing I ever heard of. I don't know how to thank you except to say thank you.

And now something you will get a big kick out of. Yesterday was our last day of school. On Monday, the 20th, Miss Starr, the principal, asked my mother to let me out of my room and let *her* decide on the punishment. Guess what it was? I wasn't allowed to ride the school bus for the last week of school.

What a punishment!

June 26, 1938

Dear Mrs. Roosevelt,

I have three letters in a row and I was wondering if you could put them in the Eleanor basket next to President Roosevelt for me because then I could mail three letters with just one stamp.

That would be very nice of you if you could do that for me, Mrs. Roosevelt.

It's all right with me if you read the letters too.

I hope you are okay.

Love from your friend,
Hannah

June 26, 1938

Dear Mr. Harry Hopkins,

I am enclosing this in a letter to Mrs. Roosevelt to put in the Eleanor basket for President Roosevelt. This is how I save stamps. My mother says, "Three cents is three cents."

Why I am writing is to thank you for the WPA.

My father says he read in the papers that you are the main man in charge and that you said about artists, "An artist has to eat too." So I wanted to thank you because we met an artist who was so poor he didn't have anything to eat and we gave him a cheese sandwich and a cup of coffee and a piece of pie à la mode. He painted a picture of a fireplace for us to put next to our radio for when President Roosevelt gives a fireside chat. The next day he got on a train and rode all across the country till he found a WPA job in a logging camp in Oregon. And now he has a job as an artist again in the WPA. My mother said maybe that means hard times are improving a little bit. He is only one man, but when we met him he was poor and couldn't work and had nothing to eat and now he's working and more than that—he's doing the work he loves. My mother said one man is very important. I think so too.

I think *you* must be very important if this was your idea.

Your friend,
Hannah Diamond

P.S. My teacher's name is Miss Dorothy Hopkins. Are you related to her?

June 26, 1938

Dear President Roosevelt,

Hello, it's me again!

I finally met two of those people you said don't like you!

They were customers. They were very fancy. The lady had a fur piece with a fox's nose at the end. They had a chauffeur, like Madame Chiang Kai-shek had!

They got into an argument with my father and mother—about you! They didn't call you by your proper name.

They said you were a traitor to your class. They said you should think a little more about the upper class and a little less about the lower class.

My father said, "This is the United States, not England. We don't have classes."

The man said, "The customer is always right."

My father said, "Except when he's wrong."

The lady snapped the fox's nose at the end of her fur piece and said, "We shall take our business elsewhere."

My *mother* said, "Take it to the Waldorf-Astoria!"

Everybody got so excited. The chauffeur smiled at me.

Love from your friend,
Hannah

P.S. But I still like you just the way you are.

And I am saving six cents because I am putting this and a note to Mr. Harry Hopkins inside a letter to Mrs. Roosevelt to put in the Eleanor basket.

June 26, 1938

Dear Miss Missy,

I didn't see cherry blossoms like you did in Washington, D.C., but guess what's blooming in a little glass of water on my desk in my room today?

An *apple* blossom!

Love,
Hannah

P.S. I am putting this and a letter to President Roosevelt and a letter to Mr. Harry Hopkins in a letter to Mrs. Roosevelt to go in the Eleanor basket. I am saving nine cents in all.

June 27, 1938

Dear Edward,

I forgot to tell you something: I hope you'll keep writing to me even though school is over. I certainly am going to keep writing to you. Writing is how I talk. If I can't talk, I'll explode!

Love from your friend,
Hannah

P.S. Hooray for summer—whenever I'm not helping in the restaurant, I can run up to my secret place at the top of the mountain and read books all day long!

June 27, 1938

Dear Hannah,

I hope you keep writing letters to me even though school is over. I will read all your letters to Mathilda and Hannah Junior. And then I will write back.

Your friend,
Edward

P.S. Hooray for summer—I still have to get up five o'clock in the morning to do chores but I don't have to read no more books till September!

ELEANOR ROOSEVELT

June 30, 1938

Dear Hannah,

First let me tell you that I loved your poem ''Colors.'' And thank you for drawing the violets and for remembering that they are my favorite flower.

And now I have three messages:

One: President Roosevelt said to thank you for liking him just the way he is. He was so pleased that he picked out a special stamp for you, not with an animal this time, but with a star from the Sandwich Islands. It is enclosed.

Two: Mr. Harry Hopkins said to tell you he was delighted with your note. And even though he is not related to your teacher, he wishes he was.

Three: Missy says to tell you an apple blossom is as good as a cherry blossom.

I am sending you a letter received by President Roosevelt last October from a girl in San Antonio, Texas. My good secretary, Miss ''Tommy'' Thompson, was kind enough to typewrite a copy of the original letter, which was handwritten. In this letter, the girl, Ernestine Guerrero, tells how she came to make and send something to President Roosevelt. I wish that you could see it, for it is a beautiful work of art. It is a carved wooden clock case, so large it looks like a tower. When you read her letter, you will be surprised to learn what she made it <u>from.</u> Since you and Ernestine are fellow artists, it occurred to me that perhaps she might be someone you would like to get in touch with as a possible pen pal and friend.

Love from your fellow book lover,

Eleanor Roosevelt

P.S. Also, here is a poem by our special friend Emily. It seems just the appropriate answer to the ''upper class/lower class'' remarks made by the customer whom your mother directed to the Waldorf-Astoria:

The pedigree of honey
Does not concern the bee ;
A clover, any time, to him
Is aristocracy.

October 17, 1937
San Antonio, Texas

Mr. Franklin D. Roosevelt
Washington, D. C.

Dear Sir:

About six years ago my father was helped by the Relief Organization that you originated. I always saved the wooden boxes in which the groceries came, for my father is a carpenter. He always said that we should be thankful to you for what we received. So one day I told him that I wished I could do something to show you our appreciation and he said, ''Why don't you build something pretty out of those boxes for him?'' I started working day by day for one year until I learned how, and then another year to finish what I am sending you (The Chimes of Normandy). This is the best I have ever done in my life. I know that you have many pretty things, but please accept and keep this piece of work from a poor girl that doesn't have anything, also to show you how much we admire you not only as the President of the United States but as a man of great ideals and a big heart toward humanity.

Respectfully yours,
Ernestine Guerrero
#3 Loop Street
San Antonio, Texas

July 3, 1938

Dear Mrs. Roosevelt,

Thank you for the messages and the letter. Please tell President Roosevelt the stamp he sent is my favorite.

About the poem you sent—I liked it. I tried to write one about a bee too, but it wasn't good. So I wrote about a butterfly instead:

> A butterfly came once to tea
> And landed on a flower.
> It ate and drank
> And flapped its wings
> And stayed for half an hour.
> Before it left—
> Would you believe—
> It sat a minute on my sleeve!

My mother said she read an article that said you once had your own school and you were the teacher. I wish you still had that school and I could go to it. I would love to have you for a teacher! (This is not an insult to Miss Hopkins, who is very nice even though she is not related to Mr. Harry Hopkins who made the WPA, but all the same I *would* love to have you for a teacher.)

Because, Mrs. Roosevelt, I think you are the most wonderful lady in the world. When I grow up, I would like to be just like you.

And thank you for the letter from that girl Ernestine Guerrero who made President Roosevelt the beautiful carved wooden clock case. I couldn't get over her letter.

She would be such a good friend for somebody. I would like to tell her so and I will—someday. But not today.

Because today I was reading my mother's scrapbook of "My Day" (*your* "My Day")—there are new columns in that scrapbook and old ones too—and the one I read that I liked best of all was when you said this: "I could not help but think how fortunate we are when we have real friends, people we can count on and turn to and who are always glad to see us when we are lonely."

And it made me realize something, Mrs. Roosevelt: I already have a friend!

His name is Edward.

Author's Note

This is a book of fiction. Children have asked me, "Did that really happen?" or "Was that real or did you make it up?" While fiction is made up from a writer's imagination, there is much in it that *is* real.

In this book, for example, Ernestine Guerrero's letter to President Roosevelt is real. Her original hand-written letter and the carved clock case she made for the president may be seen at the Museum of the Franklin D. Roosevelt Library in Hyde Park, New York, where the helpful staff made me a copy of the letter and later sent me a picture of the work.

President Franklin D. Roosevelt's and Eleanor Roosevelt's shared concern for poor and unemployed people was real. Their determination to do something about it was real. The WPA was real.

"The Other Franklin," as Franklin Elliot, the WPA artist in the book, calls himself, is made up (but the Grand View Restaurant was real, and unemployed men like him really did stop off and ask for—and get—something to eat). The sketch of loggers at work sent to Hannah on a postcard from this imaginary artist was inspired by a real WPA mural painted by a real-life artist named Waldo Pierce. Originally painted for a post office in Westbrook, Maine, in the 1930s, it is now installed at the Portland Museum of Art in Portland, Maine.

Eleanor Roosevelt really was an admirer of the poet Emily Dickinson, so much so that when asked by President Roosevelt to name four people she considered to be outstanding leaders, Emily Dickinson's name was one of the four.

The cherry tree that Eleanor sat in as a girl, where she hid from grown-ups and read all the books she wanted to read while eating cherries, was real.

President Roosevelt really was a dedicated stamp collector. The stamps illustrated in this book are real, though they are not from the president's albums.

The letters to and from the Roosevelts and Hannah were made up out of my imagination, as was most of the rest of the book.

Everybody has an imagination, and that is a fact.

Writers just use theirs a little more.

Acknowledgments

I would like to thank the following friends for giving me these books and materials:

Nina Metz, my daughter, who gave me *No Ordinary Time* by Doris Kearns Goodwin;

Donya Van Buren, who gave me *Eleanor, Volume 1* by Blanche Wiesen Cook;

Edward Johanson, who gave me material about the art of the New Deal, from a Franklin and Eleanor Roosevelt Institute he attended; and

Barbara Barrett, who gave me *Eleanor* by Barbara Cooney.

Other books I used were:

Eleanor Roosevelt's ***My Day,*** *1930–1945*, edited by Rochelle Chadakoff, with an introduction by Martha Gellhorn;

FDR's Fireside Chats, edited by Russell D. Buhite and David W. Levy;

A New Deal for Public Art: Murals from Federal Work Programs, published in conjunction with the exhibition of the same name, by the Bronx Museum of the Arts; and

The Complete Poems of Emily Dickinson, edited by Thomas H. Johnson.

I would also like to thank:
My son, Mark Elliot Skolsky, for helping with the drawings and giving me lessons on perspective;
My good neighbor, Chippie Deutzman, for wearing out her Xerox machine making copies for me over a period of four years;
My friend Irene Johanson, for little trees, plants, clocks, food, and all sorts of other inventive comforts;
My husband, Bernard M. Skolsky, who took me to Hyde Park (twice) and the Portland Museum of Art (twice), proofread, made phone calls, dated the letters, numbered the pages, loaned me his stamp album from the 1930s—and listened;
My therapist, Selwyn J. Pereira, M.D., for encouraging me to "let yourself be the person that you are";
My grandson, Zachary Harrison Metz, for bringing back my joie de vivre;
And special thanks to my most unusual editor and friend, Richard W. Jackson, for teaching me how to make music.